# THE ROADSTER PROJECT

A Novel

## Tom Glosser

# THE ROADSTER PROJECT

A Novel

## Tom Glosser

SUNSTONE
PRESS

SANTA FE

Sunstone books may be purchased for educational, business, or sales promotional use.
For information please write: Special Markets Department, Sunstone Press,
P.O. Box 2321, Santa Fe, New Mexico 87504-2321.

Book and Cover design > Vicki Ahl
Body typeface > Corbel
Printed on acid free paper

Library of Congress Cataloging-in-Publication Data

Glosser, Tom, 1939-
The roadster project : a novel / by Tom Glosser.
    p. cm.
ISBN 978-0-86534-831-8 (softcover : alk. paper)
1. Antique and classic cars--Collectors and collecting--Fiction. I. Title.
PS3607.L67R63 2011
813'.6--dc23

                    2011029616

**WWW.SUNSTONEPRESS.COM**

SUNSTONE PRESS / POST OFFICE BOX 2321 / SANTA FE, NM 87504-2321 /USA
(505) 988-4418 / ORDERS ONLY (800) 243-5644 / FAX (505) 988-1025

This story is dedicated to all who appreciate old cars. To those car lovers who provide a home for these old-timers, as measured in car-years. And to those who actually toil at bringing them back from the brink. Would that there were more stories, fact or fiction, about such people and their dream cars.

# 1

Ten year old Marty Gibson stood in the middle of the street and watched as his uncle drove off to New Jersey and a new job. The youngster felt only affection for his uncle, but the tears were not about him. He'd promised to return occasionally, but failed to include his Roadster.

The boy was convinced this was the last time he would ever see the old car. When it was out of sight, he hooked his thumbs in the back pockets of his jeans and slowly returned to the sidewalk. "Some day," he vowed, in a barely audible voice. "Some day."

Dejected by the loss of man and machine, he sat down on the curbstone and recalled memories of happier times. Two years earlier, during 1943, Uncle Walt returned from the war with part of his foot missing. He'd come to Carlisle, to reacquaint himself with this branch of his family and to work at his brother's auto repair garage.

Marty spent part of that afternoon listening to the adults talk and the rest of the time outside, circling his uncle's car. He was crazy about cars, especially the older ones. Until that day, he'd never been aware of the existence of 1936 Ford Roadsters. This one was black, with whitewall tires and a tan canvas top. Hands down, it was the most terrific car he'd ever seen.

The youngster got to spend many hours in the Roadster. The deep, powerful growl of its V-8 engine, the gently curved dashboard and the feel of its leather seat, intoxicated him. Topping all, was the car's looks. From any angle, it was a knockout. In no time, Marty developed a deep affection for the car and had mistakenly assumed it would be a part of his life forever.

A month or so after leaving, Uncle Walt returned from New Jersey for an afternoon visit and to show off his new car. Marty never asked about the Roadster. In car years, it was quite old and learning its fate would have likely reopened his wounds. The grieving, moping, anger and emptiness wounds he'd mostly overcome.

Later that day, after supper, he called out, "Mom, I'm going out for a while."

John put down the newspaper and said, "Wait up, Son, I'll go with you." He'd noticed Marty's dispirited behavior since the absence of his brother's Roadster. Earlier today, learning the old car no longer belonged to his uncle, had to be hard on his boy.

They were overdue for a talk. On that early autumn evening, the two walked past several houses in silence, before John spoke.

"Marty, I want you to be aware of something. I think I know how much your uncle Walt's Roadster meant to you."

"Yeah, it was some car, huh, Dad?" John nodded.

"I'm going to get my own Roadster, when I'm old enough to drive."

"Son, that might be more difficult than you think. There might not be many around by then. Heck, there weren't that many around in 1936. I've seen very few of them over the years."

"I've only seen one."

"You know, for that reason, I gave a lot of thought to buying that car and storing it away in the garage."

Marty stopped walking. "Really, Dad? Why didn't you?"

"Well, it wasn't all that simple. People change, Son. Their interests change, especially the interests of young fellas like yourself. Who knows if you'd even give a hoot about that car six years from now."

"Oh, I'd have given a hoot."

"Yes, I've come to believe you would."

"Trouble is, what am I going to use for money to buy my car when the time comes? I thought a lot about it. Delivering newspapers or boxing groceries aren't the answer, even if I did both. I need a real job." He inhaled deeply. "Dad, is there any chance you'd hire me at the garage? Is there some kind of work I can do?"

"Well, what about school?"

"After school and Saturdays and all summer."

"Couldn't a job wait a few years, Marty?"

"All I'm asking for is a chance, Dad. I can handle school and a job. Please, let me give it a try, won't you?"

In a way, John liked that his son wasn't taking his recent setback in stride. But the idea of his ten year old boy working at a job, even part-time, was something else again. They walked past several houses before he answered.

"We'll see, buddy. Don't say anything about this until I have a chance to talk it over with your mom." Then, playfully, he grabbed Marty and rubbed his knuckles through the boy's hair.

The following week Marty showed up after school and worked a few hours each day at the garage. Mostly he swept up, cleaned spills and generally kept the garage orderly.

When he received his first pay envelope, his mother took him to their bank to open a savings account and make his first deposit.

At the kitchen table that evening, he proudly showed his father the bankbook. On the cover, Marty had printed, THE ROADSTER PROJECT.

During those first few months at the garage, Marty became a favorite of the three mechanics his father employed. They recognized his eagerness to learn and his surprising work ethic and, one by one, they became his mentors.

Over the ensuing years, he gave his dad plenty to smile about. He learned quickly and, before long, was doing more and more demanding work at the garage. In time he was capable of doing engine tune-ups, provided he could stand on a wooden box. At sixteen, he was doing engine and transmission rebuilds.

Marty was a natural and John lit up with pride when a satisfied customer referred to his son as a chip off the old block. Some even asked for him when they brought their cars in for repair.

Time passed and, one night at the dinner table, Marty handed the bankbook to his father.

"I've got enough in there to buy a brand new car, Dad, so I'm sure it's enough for my Roadster."

John flipped through the many pages and years of deposits. He was struck by the fact he didn't find a single withdrawal entry. As John shook his head, he said, "Seventeen years old. Good work, Son. You've done it. You should be very proud of yourself. God knows your mom and I are as proud of you as we can be."

From then on Marty would no longer accept payment for his work at the garage. Not to be outdone, John bought a customer's 1951 Ford Coupe, a car his son had long admired.

Mechanically, the car needed a good deal of work. Father and son stayed after the shop closed for the day to put the car in a safe and dependable condition. Those many hours and evenings together were the stuff of golden memories for both Gibsons.

Marty put the car to good use during the countless hours spent searching for a Roadster and, later, on those long commutes to and from college most weekends.

While he'd been away fulfilling his military obligation, his dad built a first class car hauling trailer for him. When he returned from the service, for good, he still used the '51 Ford as his daily transportation, but it was unsuited for trailer towing.

Before long, he'd located a 1956 Chevy Nomad station wagon and made the purchase.

Its like new outward appearance contradicted the many miles it had logged. Still, it was a good buy and Marty modified it to meet his needs. The Nomad and trailer had not failed him during any of his consistently unrewarding weekend and annual searching trips.

# 2

1961

$S$tate trooper Marty Gibson had been on patrol all morning, stopping briefly in town after town to insure all was well. Small towns, farms and an occasional saw mill made up his extensive area of responsibility in north-central Pennsylvania.

At the next town, Lanier, he'd be having lunch with Margie. She'd left her job at a high powered law firm in New York and returned to the family farm when her father suffered a mild heart attack. She helped care for him, pitched in to work the farm and landed a part-time job with the local attorney. She and Marty had met soon after her arrival and it hadn't taken long for their affection for each other to grow into love.

So far, she'd been tolerant of his being obsessed with the idea of finding an old car and his frequent absences while he searched for it. However, when she'd called last night, asking him to meet her for lunch, he had the feeling her patience was wearing thin. He wasn't looking forward to lunch.

Entering Lanier, he noticed her car in front of the diner, but his attention shifted to a large black sedan parked illegally in front of the bank. The sedan's lone occupant seemed intensely interested in the new arrival. Marty could see vapors coming from the sedan's exhaust on that cold January day.

Frowning, he parked the patrol car at an angle, for protection, then stepped out into the street. As he reached for his mobile phone, three men burst through the bank's doors and spotted the state police car.

"Police! Stop right there," he shouted.

The response was a series of shotgun blasts which rattled nearby windows and ripped into the patrol car. He returned fire, hitting the man carrying the canvas bank bag. The others quickly helped their associate to his feet and into the car.

Crouching by the front wheel of his car, Marty reloaded his revolver. He looked up to see people inside the diner, most crowding the large plate glass window. Margie, closest to the door, was being restrained.

"Get away! Get back!" Marty yelled, while gesturing.

In the distance, someone yelled, "Let's get the hell out of here!" Car doors slammed.

As he stood up, the sound of screeching tires drowned out the engine's roar. He holstered his weapon while watching the car race off down the main street and turn onto State Route 19. They were headed for the nearby New York state line.

Speeding off in pursuit, he grabbed the phone and called his headquarters. The response was garbled because of the great distance involved. Next, he called the sheriff's office. No units were nearby, but the dispatcher would alert their people and the state police.

He tossed the phone onto the seat and focused on keeping the black sedan in sight. The high powered patrol car soon closed the gap, but remained out of shotgun range.

Both cars were flying along the narrow country road, at times reaching eighty miles an hour. Marty glanced at the rear view mirror and saw white smoke coming from his car. The temperature gauge needle was nearly pegged. The radiator had taken a hit during the gunfire exchange and the engine had begun to misfire.

While trying to figure out what he might do, the brake lights of the sedan unexpectedly glared and tire smoke obliterated his view of the car. Though he got on his brakes, the patrol car skidded into shotgun range.

When the smoke cleared, glass was broken out of the sedan's rear window and shotgun barrels appeared. He threw himself across the seat just as windshield fragments filled his car. During the next barrage, the hood flew up as he ducked.

As the sedan raced off, the patrol car rolled lifelessly to a stop. He stood in the middle of the road and watched the sedan until it was little more than a speck. Then another surprise, the sedan's taillights flashed and the car turned off the road.

Returning to his car, he found the radiator jammed into the fan. He finally got the two separated. The hood had also been damaged and wouldn't stay closed, so he jerked it from side to side until the hinge on the driver's side broke free. While looking behind to see if the sedan had gotten back on the highway, he yelled, "Come on, give!" The other hinge wouldn't break off, so he twisted the hood around until it was draped over the passenger fender, almost touching the ground.

Hurriedly, he got in and tried to start the engine. Amidst ear splitting screeching sounds and vibrations, the car began to roll. Twenty miles an hour, that was its top speed. Sparks from the battery and a pungent smell from the engine collected inside the car, through the vast windshield opening.

Nearing the turnoff, his hand covered his left eye as searing pain blinded him. "Damn!" He suspected it must be glass which was all over the dashboard. Out came the handkerchief and he flapped it open. Sure that it was glass free, he held it gently to his eye. The pain had become tolerable by the time he pulled onto the dirt road and stopped.

After calling in his location and status, he drove along the dirt road. He had to know if there was a back way out of here. One hundred yards in there was a large clearing with a farmhouse, barn and a few sheds. The dirt road ended at the barn. He watched as the barn doors opened and another sedan rolled out. It would be coming his way shortly.

He shifted into reverse and chugged back out toward the paved road. By now, the engine was making all sorts of noises and the car shuddered violently. With the country road only twenty yards away, there was a flash and single muffled explosion, before his car fell silent and motionless. Tall narrow trees, with limbs only near their tops, encased the dirt passageway, now blocked by his vehicle.

After removing the shotgun and shells from the trunk, he paused long enough to look into the outside rear view mirror. There was blood along the edge of his eyelid. He quickly crossed the highway and took up a defensive position behind a sizable boulder, then waited and worried about his injury. When the hell is help going to get here? he wondered. I'm freezing my ass off.

Freezing became the least of his concerns when he saw the sedan coming toward him along the dirt road. The car stopped some distance away once the driver saw the smoldering hulk blocking the exit. Three men got out and, after a brief huddle, split up. They were going to attack from three directions. He double checked his weapons.

Moments later, from the direction of Lanier, he saw vehicles approaching. Two pickup trucks loaded with men slowed and pulled off the road when they saw Marty.

Eleven men with rifles piled out of the trucks.

"You can't imagine how glad I am to see you fellas," he said. While they kept out of sight behind the trucks, he filled them in on the situation.

"What happened to your eye?" one of the men asked.

He waved off the question without answering.

"Maybe you should wait here while we go flush out that scum in there," another man said. There were murmurs of agreement all around. "Wait. Hold it, fellas. Who lives in that farmhouse back in there?"

"Nobody. That's the old Garner place. They been gone for years," said another.

"Okay." Marty took a deep breath. "Look, we've got them trapped. Let's wait for them to come to us. Let's not back them into a corner and force a fight."

The men thought it made good sense. At Marty's direction, they fanned out along the roadway to watch for anyone trying to escape. Sirens sounded in the distance, coming from opposite directions. Two state police cars and one from the sheriff's force converged. Soon after, the road was cordoned off.

After Marty briefed the new arrivals, a trooper took charge. Comfortable with their situation, he told his colleague to get Marty into town for medical attention. Holding the handkerchief to his eye, he stood there, looking across the road at the sorry state of his patrol car. Smoke still billowed from its engine compartment. He turned to the trooper beside him. "Looks like my car is going to the scrapyard, Ed."

Ed called ahead to Lanier and was told the doctor was out on a emergency and they should go directly to the hospital in Jensen.

Removing his jacket at the hospital, Marty discovered he'd also been shot in the arm. Actually, as gunshot wounds go, his barely bled. However, he growled at the sight of two holes in the sleeve and the ruin of a practically new jacket.

After treatment, and because of the lateness of the day, the doctor wanted him to remain overnight for a follow-up eye examination in the morning.

Once settled in his room, a short parade of well wishers visited. Margie was not among them. She had waited until the others had left.

The first thing out of her mouth was, "Oh, Marty, not your eye!"

"It's fine, Angel. What felt like half a soda bottle turned out to be a speck of glass. It's been removed and this eye-patch will go in a day or two. After that, eye-drops for a few days and I'm a hundred percent."

"The robbery is all they're talking about on the radio. They say you were shot."

"It's nothing, really. The needle I got a little while ago hurt more." He slapped his upper arm and rotated it vigorously to confirm his claim. "I'm only here to cut down on unnecessary travel, that's all."

Margie looked relieved. She turned to make sure no one was within hearing distance. "My timing is just awful."

He was pretty sure of what was coming, but asked anyway. "What timing is that?"

She hesitated, organizing her thoughts. "Remember I told you that my old boss has been calling, asking me to return to work in New York City?" Before he could respond, she added, "Yesterday, I told him I would."

"When? When are you going?"

"In a few hours."

"You're calling it quits?"

"No, nothing of the kind! It's just, Sweetheart, my dad is fine now. I only came back to help out. My job in town with Mister Adams has all but dried up. There simply isn't much work for lawyers around here and even less for legal secretaries. Marty, he hasn't had a single client in the past month. I can't take any more of his money."

"But, what about us, Margie?"

"Oh, Marty, I don't know. I love you, but I feel like I'm competing against that rainbow you're chasing. I understand how important it is for you to find that car, but how many more years will it take?"

Just then, three state trooper friends came into the room. He forced a smile and motioned for them to give him a few minutes.

"This isn't an ultimatum, believe me. I'm not even sure I'm doing the right thing. I'm not sure of anything anymore. Marty, I'm twenty-three years old. I'll wait for you, but at some point..." Her eyes filled with tears, as she whispered, "Find our car, Marty. Just find it, so we can get on with our lives."

She wrapped her arms around him and whispered, "I love you." She kissed him, ran her hand through his hair and stared at him for a moment, then quietly left the room.

Marty grabbed the pillow from his bed and threw it against the wall. "Damn!"

Two of his friends came into the room, smiling. The third was still out in the hallway, watching Margie's every step. When she was out of sight, he joined the others.

"What a doll! She's crazy about me, no doubt about it," he teased.

The four men talked for some time, mostly about his injuries and his robbery experience. Then, as they were leaving, his boss showed up. After completing some reports, the sergeant stood up.

"Damned glad you came out of this so well, Marty. That was a tough spot to be in, for a rookie. Call me tomorrow, when they spring you, and I'll get you a ride."

Vince started toward the door and stopped.

"I want you to take some time off." He thought a second and said, "Report for duty on Saturday. That'll give you a little time to ease back in."

"But that isn't—"

Vince was already shaking his head. "Saturday, unless there's a complication."

Late the following morning, Marty was packing some things for a visit with his folks down in Carlisle, when his boss, Vince, came into the barracks.

"Glad I caught you. Just got a call. A Captain Wilson wants to meet with you in Harrisburg. Tomorrow morning, ten sharp."

"What about, Sarge?"

"They didn't say and I didn't ask." Seeing the concern on Marty's face, he added, "I don't think there's a problem. Still, I'd wear my uniform, if I were you."

"Right, Sarge. Thanks."

He prepared carefully for his meeting the next morning. He'd never even seen a Captain, let alone met one. It made him a bit nervous, as did the nagging feeling he might be in some kind of trouble. Why else would he be summoned?

Marty showed up for the meeting in uniform, on time and in parade condition. At six feet tall and one-hundred eighty pounds, not even the eye-patch spoiled his good looks.

Wilson was on the phone when Marty was led into his office. He motioned to the trooper to take a seat. Wilson looked and sounded more like a weather-beaten old sea captain than a big shot cop, Marty thought.

When the call ended, Wilson studied the young man for a moment.

"You Gibson?"

"Yes, sir."

The captain walked around the desk, still watching him, and sat on a corner of it. He reached back and picked up a folder.

"Says here, you're twenty-six. Marine Corps and a college graduate." His eyes shifted to his visitor for confirmation.

"Yes, sir. I've been out of the academy almost eleven months."

"You're a regular bulldog, aren't you?"

Uh oh, he thought, here it comes.

Without waiting for an answer, Wilson said, "How about you tell me what happened during that robbery, start to finish. Mostly, I want to know your thinking."

Marty measured his words carefully at first, recounting the facts of the incident. Then outlined his actions.

"From the start, sir, it was my intention to dog the subjects, nothing more. I wasn't about to wait around for ten or twenty minutes for backup to show. They'd be long gone. That gunfight on the town's main street, Captain, I didn't have a choice. They opened up on me as soon as they saw my car. Maybe—"

"Wait. Hold on a minute. You think you've been called on the carpet?"

No response.

"You know why you're here, Gibson?"

"No, sir."

"Dammit to hell! There's been some kind of foul up. I apologize. This is a job interview. You did first rate police work up there in wherever the hell that place is. Those boys been bouncing back and forth between New York and here, robbing small banks for damn near two years. Thanks in large part to you, we're the ones who got them."

Marty began to relax.

"We okay to move on?"

"Yes, sir."

"Okay, here it is, my pitch," Wilson began. "We got trouble out in the southwestern part of the state, south of Pittsburgh. Truckers. Bunch of them are way out of line. It's been festering for too long and it's getting worse."

Wilson stood up and began pacing.

"They're racing as if the highways were their private domain. Some innocent people have been killed. They've even run some of our guys right the hell off the road. That's how bad it is."

He stopped talking and took a deep breath.

"I'm putting together a team of troopers, strictly volunteer, you understand. They'll reinforce the area and help put things right." He paused to study Marty.

"You're a bit young, but dammit, I want you on my team, Gibson. That's why you're here. Don't know how long the job will take. I'm guessing three to four months. Only thing for sure is, there'll be a lot of hours, including weekends. Damn little time off, if any."

Only the action this job would bring was enticing, however, there was a prize in this package. Wilson threw out the bait.

"When the job's finished, you can choose any location in the state for your next assignment. I guarantee it." He waited for Marty to absorb this. "Well, how about it?"

"Where do I sign up, Captain?"

Wilson looked pleased.

Thinking he would be pressed into service immediately, he motioned to his eye and asked, "What about this, Captain?"

"Not a problem," Wilson replied, as he wrote something on a form and handed an envelope to his recruit. "You're in my unit, as of now. Take some time, rest up and I'll see you out there on the thirtieth. It's all there in the envelope."

Marty was all smiles, when he left the office. What a break! Over two weeks off!

As soon as he could locate a phone, he called home. "Mom, I've been transferred. Right now I'm going up to the barracks to collect my things. I'll probably be back before Dad gets home."

That evening, during dinner, he told his parents about his new assignment and the time off.

"Apparently it'll take a few weeks to fill out the team," he said.

"Nonsense," John said. "It's a reward and you deserve it."

"Your father's right, Marty."

Smiling, John got up from the table and patted his son on the shoulder as he passed by. Moments later, he returned, handing Marty a bankbook before taking his seat.

"Where to this time, Son?"

"California. Finally, I've got the time."

"Oh, Marty. So far? At this time of year. In this weather?" his mother said.

"I can't believe this," John said. "Alice, our son is a state trooper. You do know he's driven on snow and ice before, don't you?" He rolled his eyes.

"But, why so far, why not—"

"Why not Wisconsin or Minnesota?" Marty interrupted. "They're a lot closer and I haven't searched there yet. Maybe I could learn to ski while I'm up that way. I'd have plenty of opportunities," he said, tongue in cheek. Then he winked at his dad.

"Look, Mom, here's why California. Of the eleven western states, California has more cars on the road than the combined total of the other ten, and—"

"What does Margie think about this?" she asked.

"I didn't tell her." Seeing the confusion on his mother's face, he mumbled, "She got tired of waiting, Mom. She's gone back to New York."

"Oh, dear, not Margie, too," she said. "She's the perfect girl for you. I was so sure you two were destined to spend your lives together." Then came the predictable sigh.

"She's right, Son. Margie's the pick of the litter."

"I couldn't agree more. But what was I to do, ask her to marry me? What would become of the Project? I can't leave her behind, while I go traipsing all over the country. And then what? Complications. If she can't go, I won't go. Or, we can't afford ... I want to be thrilled, when the news comes that I'm going to be a father. No, I won't paint myself into a corner. The Project's not going to die a slow death, or a quick one. Don't you see? This is my best chance ever. I've got a good feeling about this trip. This could be the one."

Focusing on his mother, he said, "Once the Project is closed, I'm making a beeline for New York City. If Margie was meant to be, you'll have your storybook ending, Mom. So will I."

Over coffee, John asked, "When you figure on setting out?"

"Well, it depends. I've got to check on the Nomad, trailer and the weather."

"They're ready to go. No problem there. But, according to the paper, a storm is brewing." John turned and reached for the paper, then handed it across the table.

"How long you think it'll take to get there, Son?"

"If the weather holds off, about four days. Then a week to search and another four days back. That should leave a little time to spare."

After checking the weather map, he turned to be sure his mother wasn't within earshot. "Looks like, if I left tomorrow, by mid-morning, I just might beat that storm, Dad."

"Let's go and get your trailer hooked up."

# 3

After breakfast Marty hugged his parents and after a stop at the bank headed for the Pennsylvania Turnpike. Snow flurries had begun last night and continued this morning. Nuisance snow, he called it. The genuine article was approaching from the West, along a broad front.

Once the Nomad wagon was up to cruising speed, he turned the radio on and got comfortable. Many hours passed and his adrenalin rush kept going.

Ohio was worse than when he left home. The flurries were a bit heavier and cars were driving with their lights on although it was early in the afternoon. Still, the roads were clear and he was making good time.

Parts of U.S. Route 40 had been converted to the Interstate Highway System. When the system was complete, it would allow state to state travel without red lights or stop signs. Unfortunately, the system was in the early stages of development. So far, Marty was only on the Interstate sections for very brief periods, in West Virginia and, again, here in Ohio.

By evening, he'd reached Illinois, but the weather was little changed. The latest weather reports were cautioning that heavy snow across a wide area was imminent.

Elvis began to sing, "Are You Lonesome Tonight?" for at least the fifth time since he'd left Carlisle. He was sure he knew all the lyrics of the popular songs at this point. Getting restless, he turned off the radio and tried to find a comfortable sitting position. Clearly, the huge adrenalin rush from this morning had vanished.

He began to watch for a place to gas-up and get some supper, in case things became bogged down on the highway.

Inside the restaurant, he met two young G.I.s who needed a ride. Ron and Jake were in the Air Force and were going to their new duty station in Oklahoma. Their car had given out a few hundred miles back and Marty offered to give them a lift to St. Louis.

"Until I met you fellas, my plan was to stop overnight in St. Louis and take my chances with the snow tomorrow. But, if you guys are still willing to help with the driving, we could go straight on to Oklahoma City. You heard the radio. Heavy snow could hit us anytime now. What do you think?"

"Hell, yes," said Jake.

"I'm game," added Ron.

"Okay then, when we reach Missouri, we need to get onto U.S. Route 66. That's the most direct way to both our destinations."

He set up a rotation of two hour shifts where the driver and the one riding shotgun would spell the third man who could stretch out and sleep in back.

Heading for Missouri, Ron's curiosity got the best of him.

"What's the trailer for, Marty?"

He explained about his dream car.

"You couldn't find the right Roadster in Pennsylvania?"

"It wasn't that I was picky. There were none to be had back home, or in sixteen surrounding states. Some I visited twice. And one of them, eleven times. My Roadster might have been there, but damned if I could find it. So this time it's California, or bust."

"But, all the way to California?"

"Finally, California. It's a natural."

"Why not Florida? That's closer, right?"

"It is, but the lower half of California is pretty arid. Cars rust slower and the climate is mild. If there's a Roadster haven, that has to be it. Ford probably sold a bunch of Roadsters in that part of the country. I'm banking on it. Oh, and the biggest population center in California is down south."

"Los Angeles," Ron said.

"Yep, that's it. That's my destination, greater Los Angeles. Even so, it's still going to take luck. More than I've had so far." Marty smiled. "Who knows, right?"

"I hope you luck out, Marty. Damn, what a blast! Wish I was going with you."

After stopping for gas and a change of drivers, Marty rotated to the back and fell into a deep and restful sleep. When he felt the car slowing, he propped himself up on his elbows. The sun was just coming up and the sky looked mostly clear. The Chevy was stopping alongside gas pumps.

"Where are we?" he asked.

"About fifty miles into Oklahoma," Jake said.

"Why didn't you guys call me?"

"No need," Jake said. "You'll need sleep more than us."

While the car was being refueled, Marty opened the hood to check the oil. The two younger men watched.

"What year Corvette engine is this, Marty?" Ron asked.

"Nineteen fifty-nine. I swapped in the engine and four speed out of a two month old wreck."

"This is one bitchin' ride," Jake said.

After each of them took a turn in the restroom washing up, and with Marty now behind the wheel, the questions started.

"Why is this car you're after so hard to find?" Jake wanted to know. "What is it, some kind of experimental, one of a kind, thing?"

"Not at all. It's just that Ford built a measly four thousand Roadsters in nineteen thirty-six. A drop in the bucket, compared to the hundreds of thousands of other body styles Ford cranked out that year. Even the Cabriolet outsold the Roadster by ten thousand that year."

"Cabriolet?" Jake asked.

"That was Ford's other two-door convertible. The Cabriolet was the typical convertible, with roll-up windows, while the Roadster used snap-in canvas curtains, with clear inserts for visibility." Marty laughed. "I learned a lot of cuss words when my uncle had to install those curtains during a sudden downpour."

"So, why not go for the Cabriolet?" Jake asked.

"There's one other big difference, fellas. From the doors back, the Roadster body was stretched. What a difference that made. They have that long swoopy tail end. Kind of like the Lincolns and Caddys of the day, on a smaller scale, of course.

"Hand me that small bag, will you, Ron?" Marty pulled out three pictures of his uncle's Roadster, pictures that had passed through hundreds, if not thousands of hands over the years.

"You said you've been to sixteen states looking for the car? Damn, how long you been at this?" Ron asked.

"It seems like forever. For the past five years I've gone off on trips that lasted about ten days, on average. But I could only swing that much time once a year. In between, I'd go off for one or two days at a time. I haunted New Jersey. I knew of a Roadster that was there once." He grimaced and then shrugged. "Finding it was a long shot."

Marty bought breakfast for his two new friends, then drove them to the main gate at their base near Oklahoma City.

His revised plan was to try for Amarillo, Texas, by nightfall. He wanted a good night's sleep, in a bed.

The next day, he crossed New Mexico and pushed into Arizona. Darkness had fallen and with it came intermittent rain and a series of large mountains. Climbing another of those behemoths, he instinctively squeezed the wheel tight when the windshield wipers suddenly began to scrape roughly across the glass. Ice!

He'd already reached the mountain crest and had begun a very long, steep descent. Without looking, his hand shot out and flipped the control lever from heat to defrost. Barely touching the brakes, the speedometer pointer indicated the car was stopped, then bounced around crazily, before settling on sixty miles an hour.

The car was gaining speed and the brakes were useless. So was the steering wheel. And now the windshield had become opaque, as had the rest of the windows. It was as if a giant wave had washed over the Chevy and instantly frozen.

Seventy-five! Eighty!

In mere seconds, Marty was covered in sweat. Millions of tiny needles were pricking him from his scalp to his toes.

Accepting that things were out of his hands, he pulled the seatbelt tighter, then folded his arms over the top of the steering wheel and leaned forward, resting his forehead against them. Then he closed his eyes.

Suddenly feeling himself being pressed down into his seat, he opened his eyes and stared at the speedometer. Fifty. Forty-five. Thirty. At twenty miles an hour, the Chevy hit something and stopped abruptly.

The engine idled quietly as Marty looked all around, trying to understand. The wipers were still uselessly clattering across the ice-covered glass. His shaking hand turned them off along with the headlights and the engine. Never before had he felt his heart thumping as it was now.

With a little difficulty, he rolled down his window. It was dark and silent outside. For a time he wondered if this might be Heaven, or worse. He opened the car door, carefully testing the road surface with his left foot. The sole of his shoe slid across ice, as slippery as a concrete garage floor coated with bearing grease.

Then heavy rains came. In minutes the ice was gone and he got out of the car. The passenger side front fender was buckled and the bumper was hooked on a guardrail post. Unable to finesse it loose, he got back in the car, put it in reverse, and jerked it free. Now the bumper-end was pointing forward.

Flashlight in hand, he got back out of the car and stood in the heavy rain, looking around, trying to understand what had happened. The Chevy was on a fairly steep incline. He figured the road he was on must have gone straight down the mountain, then right back up, and his car had gone roller coaster-like. A little lower down, the road angled to the left slightly, causing the Chevy to become docked against the guardrail post. Getting back into the car, he considered the damage a small price to pay to cross this mountain, given the alternative.

He stopped at the first motel he could find. His hands were still shaky as he filled out the registration card. He drove to his cabin, locked the door behind him, dropped his luggage and fell across the bed without even taking off his coat. Within seconds he was asleep.

On the fourth day, he crossed the California state line. The weather was clear and the sun warmed his face. But where were the palm trees? All he saw was barren land. California wasn't supposed to look like this.

Fifteen minutes later, he saw a car pulled off the road. Getting closer, it looked more like it had run off the highway. Instinctively, he slowed and stopped to investigate. Two middle-aged women were standing just off the pavement.

"Are you ladies okay?"

"Yes. I think so," the driver said, hesitantly.

Marty turned his attention to the car. A tire was flat.

"What happened?"

"I'm not sure," the driver said. "We were going along and, all at once, the car turned by itself and here we are."

He'd just finished up the tire change, when he noticed a police car, slowing to a stop.

Moving their car onto the side of the road, Marty said, "Good as new, ladies."

They thanked him and tried unsuccessfully to pay him for his help.

"Drive carefully, ma'am."

As the women drove off, the highway patrol officer held out his hand. "Pete O'Hara. You know, you sounded like a cop with that send-off."

"Yeah, I am. State police," Marty answered, with a smile.

They chatted a few minutes before Pete asked, "What's the trailer for?"

Marty told him of his quest. "You know of one for sale? In any condition?"

Pete shook his head. "Sorry, I sure don't." He tore a ticket from his pad and wrote on the back of it. "Here's my number at work. Give me a call in a day to two. I'll put the word out about the Roadster. We cover a lot of territory. You never know, something might turn up. Good luck with your search, Marty."

Underway, he frowned when he looked at his watch. Oh, well,

maybe that stop would count as a small down payment on the free pass he'd gotten last night, he hoped.

Reaching San Bernardino, the landscape changed dramatically. He saw houses with well groomed yards and enough palm trees to brighten his day. He rolled the window down and let the seventy degree temperature waft over him. How different from back home.

Next stop, Los Angeles. The adrenalin rush was back.

# 4

After a full eight hours of sleep, Marty was up early and raring to begin treasure hunting operations. During breakfast, he scoured the newspaper classifieds, but without luck.

Besides serving a good meal, the friendly waitress told him how to get to the local library. On hand when the doors opened, he spent the next part of the morning going through more classifieds. Two week's worth of newspaper back-issues led to a pair of gold strikes.

The advertisement that excited him most was, unfortunately, twelve days old. The other offering was more recent, having appeared in the paper only a few days ago.

Next, he located a huge phone book. Speed shops sell auto parts that modify automobiles, mostly in ways to go faster. After copying the addresses of a dozen speed shops he left the library.

Not very far from the library Marty pulled into a gas station to use the public phone. Besides the two prospects in the newspapers was another possibility he'd brought from home, an advertisement in the latest issue of a car magazine. There was no telling how long ago the seller had contacted the magazine. Nevertheless, the person lived in one of these cities making up greater Los Angeles and Marty planned to contact him.

After calling all three numbers without getting to talk with anyone, he walked to the gas station office where he'd spotted a '49 Mercury Coupe parked alongside the station.

Typically, young guys who pumped gas for a living were car lovers. They knew who owns every older car that comes close to being halfway interesting.

The two men chatted briefly about the Mercury before Marty told him what he was trying to find.

"A thirty-six Ford Roadster. Man, that's one sweet car, but I haven't seen one of those in quite a while. Sorry."

Before leaving the station, the attendant gave him directions to four of the closest speed shops on his list.

Young speed shop employees, like young gas station attendants and Marty, had at least one thing in common. They loved cars, especially the older ones.

For the next three hours, he visited speed shops and gas stations, hoping for a lead. At least once each hour, he tried to contact the three sellers.

Early in the afternoon, he visited a gas station attendant who did know of a '36 Ford Roadster and he scribbled up a pretty decent map.

"Yeah, I got a '36 Ford Roadster and, yes, it's for sale," the smiling gas pump jockey told him. "It's around back." Shoving the gasoline nozzle into a Plymouth, he said, "Go ahead. I'll catch up to you, once I finish up here."

Marty was almost running, when he turned the corner and saw the Roadster. "Aw, for crying out..." he groaned.

The car was customized, a process whereby the body sheet metal is altered, among other things, to enhance the car's appearance and make it unique. At least that's the theory of customizing.

He took his time and circled the car once and then a second time. He was heartsick. "How could anyone improve on the looks of a nineteen thirty-six Ford Roadster?" he muttered. "Why would anyone try?"

Recovering from the shock of seeing his beloved Roadster like this, he began another turn around the car, calculating what it would take to return the car to its original condition.

Headlights from a late thirty-something Buick were molded into the front fenders. Around back, he recognized the taillights from a '50 or '51 Pontiac. Even worse, the front and rear fenders had been molded to the body for a seamless, more contemporary look. The grille shell had endured lots of modification as well.

Only a few inches separated the bottom of its fenders from the ground. Cars were commonly lowered by enthusiasts for many years, to give the illusion they were longer than one at normal height. To get a car this low required major surgery on the frame, something nearly impossible to reverse correctly.

By now, he was mostly over the visual shock and, grudgingly, he became objective. In truth, the workmanship on this car was superb. He could see how some people might be willing to shell out their money to own it—just not him.

He returned to the front of the station and found the car owner still pumping gas.

Patiently, he sat down on the single step leading to the station office, and waited.

Once the attendant was free, the two men had a talk. Often, a guy who owns a certain older car knows of any others like his, for miles around. Such was not the case this time. However, the man did offer a gold nugget in the form of information.

"You ought to catch the Winternationals this Sunday. It's the first one ever and it's supposed to be huge."

"Winternationals?"

"Drag races—over at Pomona. Hey, you can bet your ass the parking lot will be jammed with some choice iron. Some will be for sale. If I were you, I'd think about it."

It was a great suggestion and Marty was going to do more than think about it.

Marty then went over to the public phone and made some calls. There was still no answer on the first or second call, but a woman answered on his third try.

"Yes, I'm calling about the thirty-six Roadster in the magazine ad."

"Oh, I'm sorry, but it's been sold."

"I'm very sorry to hear that."

Noting the disappointment in Marty's voice, she said, "Wait just a moment and I'll get my husband."

Her husband confirmed the sale.

"Would you know of another one?" Marty asked.

"No, I'm sorry, I don't."

"Do you think there's any chance the new owner might sell it for a quick profit," he persisted.

"Well, actually, I still have the car. The man who bought it had to go out of town on business and asked that the car stay put until he returned. I expect to be hearing from him any day now. Maybe you could stop by and have a look at it," the man suggested. "If you're still interested, I'll tell the new owner."

After leaving the filling station, he went to see the car. The magazine price was a very reasonable, nine-hundred dollars and the car was described as both complete and very original.

When Marty first saw the car, he immediately broke into a broad grin. It was parked in the backyard in the open. In his excitement to look the car over, he out-paced Ken, his host, and stopped to apologize. Ken watched as his visitor slowly circled the car, occasionally stopping to look more closely at something.

Although its paint was quite old, it had done a good job of protecting the body's precious sheet metal. He found no rust. The fenders had collected some dings but, otherwise, the body looked very straight and solid. If his memory served him correctly, this car was very close to the condition of his uncle's Roadster.

The worn and cracked leather seat had a few splits and a coil spring partly visible, but that and the fender dents doubtless helped to keep the price down. No question, this was the car he had long dreamed of finding and returning to its former glory.

Ken was standing back, watching his visitor check out the car. He was already feeling bad that Marty hadn't been the first to see it. The buyer hadn't shown the least bit of excitement over finding this car. He bought it much as a person would buy a new shirt.

Walking backward towards Ken, so as not to take his eyes off of the car, Marty said, "I'm heartbroken. I've been searching for this car for years. Even ran some ads in the local paper, off and on."

"No luck, I take it."

"Actually, there was one response. A farmer called and said he had a Roadster. I was there in a flash. He had a Roadster, all right. It was sunk to its axles in dirt and mud and probably hadn't moved in twenty years. All four fenders were rotted away up to ground level. Just about the entire body was covered in heavy rust and there were plenty of bullet holes. Probably some bored deer hunters, I imagine."

"Doesn't sound like much of a find," Ken commented.

"That's not all. The hood and engine were missing and a two foot thick tree was growing in their place. There wasn't a single thing worth saving from that poor car. Ken, would it be okay if I called you each day, until the new owner shows up?"

"Sure, that'll work."

Marty drove away, somewhat downcast. He'd located his treasure, but it was just beyond his reach. He set the odds of owning that car at about equal to his returning to New Jersey for the twelfth time and finding his uncle's Roadster.

Next up was a visit to the seventh speed shop on his list. Right off it provided another lead. A friend of a friend of this speed shop employee had a Roadster. A quick look at Marty's Roadster photos confirmed it. After several phone calls, he made contact and was invited to come by and see it.

The trip was a wild goose chase. It was a 1936 Ford convertible all right, but not a Roadster. Only Cabriolets had roll-up windows. And this one was nice. He only stayed long enough to be polite and explain what he was trying to find.

This owner was willing, but unable, to help lead him to another prospect. But, he was able to identify another of the yet to be visited speed shops on his dwindling list.

Marty located another phone. There was still no answer when he called the first number, but his next call was answered.

"I'm calling about the thirty-six Roadster," he began.

There was a slight hesitation. "Um ... yes. Uh, there's been a little mix-up on that."

"Mix-up?"

"I'm selling the car for my daughter, you see. The car belongs to her husband. She was supposed to drop off the ownership papers before leaving on a trip, but she forgot."

"When do expect her back?"

"I'm not sure. Uh, she's going through a divorce. She's got a lot on her mind. You know how those things are."

Marty's mind raced. He didn't personally know how such things were, but he did know this car had trouble written all over it.

From experience, he knew how important it was to obtain a signed, valid, ownership document. Damn! he thought. Maybe this was one of those divorces where the husband was out of the picture, or whatever, and the wife was trying to clean up, sell everything. If things were really hostile, her husband might even claim the car was stolen.

When their conversation ended, he hung up the phone and gently bumped his head against the phone booth door a few times.

Overall, this had been an exciting day and there was ample cause for optimism. In one day, he'd already equaled the number of leads turned up during his past five years of searching. That brought a smile. And, he still had one more prospect. This place really is a Roadster haven, he told himself.

# 5

After breakfast, Marty dialed the only remaining lead he had, but still no answer.

He reached for his wallet. It was time to call Pete O'Hara, the cop he'd met the other day while changing the flat tire for those two ladies.

"Did Pete O'Hara leave a message for me?"

"Hold on," the voice replied. "Got a pencil?"

"Yes, go ahead."

"You're supposed to call an Edgar Mannis." The voice recited the phone number.

Mannis is a retired cop who'd stopped by headquarters and noticed a copy of the O'Hara note on the bulletin board.

He answered on the second ring. As soon as Marty identified himself, the man began talking as if he'd rehearsed a speech.

"It was during the summer of forty-one. I cited a kid for speeding. He was driving a black thirty-six Ford Roadster. When I checked his driver's license, worked out he lived just a few streets from me, right here in Chastaine."

Wrinkles formed on Marty's forehead. The guy remembered all this twenty years after making a traffic stop? He shook his head. Pete must have put Mannis up to this.

"Anyway," Mannis continued, "after the war, there was this story in the magazine section of our Sunday paper about that same kid and his car."

Marty figured Mannis was sometimes reading from the old article.

"Seems the kid went missing, right after going overseas, early in the war. How his dad kept the car all cleaned up for him, in case he turned up. Oh, the kid's name was Benjamin.

"So I checked the phone book and, sure enough, Owens still lives on that same street."

Marty didn't know what to think. By now, Mannis should have broken out laughing and yelled, "April fools" or "Gotcha." Something.

Mannis continued. "Look, I know this is pretty old stuff, a long shot. But the way I see it, what've you got to lose by calling?" He plowed ahead with the phone number.

"You're right, Mister Mannis. Thanks for taking this time with me." He hesitated.

"Mister Mannis, you have a remarkable memory."

Mannis chuckled.

Uh oh, he thought.

"I call it a trick memory," Mannis said. "It used to win me money on bets, 'till word got around. One time, the guys I worked with brought in this book of poetry. Bet I couldn't recite this one page they picked out. So I took a look and never missed a word. Mind you, I didn't understand much of what I recited, but that wasn't the bet. The thing was, after that, the easy money dried up."

Standing in the phone booth, after the call, Marty smiled and then shook his head. He no longer doubted the validity of the Mannis call. It was just that, only yesterday, he almost passed on one of the leads from the library because it was twelve days old. Now, here he was, intrigued by a lead that was maybe twenty years old.

It was almost ten o'clock. He tried the number from the newspaper. Then he called the number Mannis had given him. Before the phone could ring, he hung up and returned to his car. He needed to give this guy Owens more thought.

After making inquiries at a number of filling stations, he'd reached Chastaine. During that span of time, he struggled over the approach to take with Owens.

Calling on the phone was a tricky proposition, he thought. It's so much easier to hang up, than it is to turn away a visitor at the door. However, just showing up at someone's door without being invited could also lead to a quick exit.

His quandary stemmed from the fact that he had no idea how to broach this subject with Owens. This time, he wished he didn't know so much about the Owens family.

Trying to get his hands on their dead son's car seemed kind of bizarre. He hoped not to say or do anything that would offend Owens. That, he concluded, was what made the situation sticky.

The issue was still unresolved, when he pulled up and parked in front of the Owens' residence.

This was another very nice neighborhood. All of the houses were set well back from the wide street and looked somewhat alike. Not that their sameness detracted in the least. It didn't. Their Spanish style, with orange colored roof tiles, actually made the neighborhood seem kind of story-book like.

After stalling for a minute, he took a deep breath and headed for the house. He climbed the four steps to a long sidewalk that led to the front porch. After ringing the doorbell, he stepped back, taking in the many palm trees that lined the street. It was a very impressive sight.

A tall, slender man, with gray hair, opened the door.

Marty spoke quickly, as if making a speech to a large group of people for the first time. His first burst was, "Good morning, I'm Marty Gibson." Without pause, he added, "I spoke with a man from the neighborhood, who—"

"Won't you come in, young fella?"

Inside, Marty found a warm and pleasant setting. After Patrick introduced himself and the two shook hands, Mary, his wife, joined them. They were a very nice couple and he could feel his tension ebbing. Soon, they were talking like old friends.

Eventually, the subject of his visit came up. At that point, Patrick stood up and excused himself. As soon as Marty mentioned the Roadster, the older man looked as if he wanted to be somewhere else. Anywhere else. He had already apologized for barging in like this. Now, he was cursing himself for not phoning these people.

Mary seemed oblivious to what had just happened.

"Would you like some coffee, or maybe something cold?" she asked.

When he didn't answer, she quietly followed her husband.

He could hear them talking in another room. They weren't arguing, exactly, but they were discussing something he couldn't quite make out. Then, the house was silent.

Moments later, the couple came back in with coffee and little cakes. He'd been struggling with the idea of leaving, but now it was too late. Besides, maybe this visit would lead somewhere.

The expression on Patrick's face was now one of embarrassment, which was a huge improvement from a few minutes ago.

"Please," he invited, "you were talking about that Roadster."

Marty gushed on about how he came to be captivated by the little car and continued with a recounting of all he'd done to find one over the years. Patrick and Mary were apparently impressed, based on the glances going on between the two while he talked.

He pretended not to notice.

"How much longer will you be out here?" Patrick asked.

"I have to be back to work by the thirtieth, sir."

Patrick was smiling and nodding. "You certainly have determination."

"Stickativity," Mary added, with an approving smile.

Things grew quiet. He noticed Mary smiling at Patrick and nodding her head.

"Yes, we still have that car," Patrick announced. "It's out back in the garage. If you're still interested, after seeing it, I'm sure we can reach an agreement."

Marty jumped to his feet. Mary went off to find the garage key.

While she was gone, Patrick made reference to the newspaper article that Mannis had spoken of earlier. "There was a parade of people who came around to buy that car afterwards, teen-agers mostly. Our son loved that car," Patrick confided. "I just couldn't sell it and see some youngster driving it around the neighborhood all banged up."

The two men walked along the driveway in brilliant sunshine, making small talk. Marty took in the details of the large, two car garage. It looked similar to the house with its stucco sides and same tiled roof. Its doors swung open, instead of lifting up, so they each took a side.

He could see a large clutter of furniture clogging the entrance to the Roadster. Beyond that, he could see only the unpainted wooden wall which divided the garage in half.

Still outside, he stood on tiptoe, attempting to get a glimpse of the Roadster. Patrick began to move a tall cabinet and Marty quickly pitched in to help. After swiping at a large spider web, Patrick motioned for him to follow and they slipped between some dusty furniture and into a very dusty garage.

Marty froze in his tracks. There was no car! Not a complete car, at any rate. Everywhere he looked there were parts of a car. Some were covered by sheets of canvas, while others had become dust magnets.

Shelving spanned the entire rear of the garage, from ceiling to floor. On the left side, shelving was configured in a large grid of cubicles. Most contained boxes and cans of various sizes. Mostly, there were cans. Cans that were once probably filled with fruit juice while some were as small as soup cans, and still other sizes that once contained who knew what.

Higher up, close to the ceiling, were a pair of headlights, peering out through another of the countless cobwebs.

Standing still, only Marty's eyes moved. They shifted to the right where large recognizable objects such as doors and fenders dangled from ropes like sides of beef in an old time meat market. Additionally, there were vertical dividers which helped to isolate the large items from each other. Above those parts were two horizontal shelves full of more things covered by canvas.

Patrick turned and looked at his visitor. "I thought it would be best for you to see for yourself."

It was difficult for Patrick to read Marty's expressionless face. He had no idea what his young visitor might be thinking.

Marty knew about cars in this condition, though not first hand. He'd heard about them over the years. They were called, "Basket Cases." The basket part referred to the car's smaller parts being collected in baskets for transfer to the new owner's garage.

Basket cases were mostly run down, rusted out, or beat-up cars, that needed to be taken apart to address their ills. They could be had cheaply. Even so, optimistic souls underestimated the extent of their defects. Then too, possibly the lack of necessary skills, knowledge or patience to complete the job, were factors. Whatever the reason, these cars, or their components, often ended up for sale.

But this basket case was out of character. So why was it taken apart like this? For what purpose? he wondered.

Reaching the vast number of cans on the rear shelves, he removed one and the paper inside. He could see the can was full of nuts and bolts, no doubt belonging to this car. The printing on the paper read, Front axle assembly." He removed other cans at random.

Some, in addition, had notations about the can's contents and a few even had crude but helpful drawings. Whoever did this had taken the time to make sure he would be able to put the car back together, at some point.

Turning back to the big items, he moved several feet to his left. There was a large mound, sitting on several four by four lengths of lumber. It was covered by a giant, plastic type table cloth, with a very soft, fuzzy underside, the kind that adorned kitchen table tops when he was just a boy.

After pulling back this covering almost its entire length, the Roadster's body dazzled him. He was stunned by the sight of the dust free, brilliant black paint. Seeing the green pinstripe, running the length of the body brought fond, boyhood memories rushing back.

Sneezing several times, because of the dust storm he'd caused, he shot a giant smile toward Patrick. Looking for signs of use, or flaws, turned up nothing on this side of the body, even after kneeling for a closer look.

The beautiful wood grained dash looked newly minted. Then his eyes fell on the odometer and once again he shot a look of joy, tempered by a touch of disbelief, toward Patrick.

"Is this mileage right?" he finally got out, between coughs.

"Yes, I'm sure it is."

"Only a little over twelve thousand miles?"

The older man smiled and shrugged his shoulders. "Yes. If that's what is says, you can be sure it's accurate."

From the moment he had pulled back the body's covering, it became clear he had just stumbled onto something very special. This car was spectacular, or at least it would be, when it was made whole. He was certain there couldn't be another one nicer than this anywhere.

Leaving the body uncovered, Marty went back to examine one of the fenders. Lightly rubbing a spot, it appeared to be as nice as the body. It seemed like he'd walked into some sort of tiny, 1936 Ford assembly plant. A plant the workers had abandoned before this car was assembled.

Judging from the size of the item covered with canvas leaning against the wall, it had to be the Roadster's frame. He peeled back the canvas to get a look. The frame had been cleaned carefully, before storage, and the lightweight canvas had done its job perfectly.

Stepping away from the frame, he put both hands up to his face. How can this be? he wondered. There he stood, between the frame and the body, with a huge smile. Then he laced his fingers on top of his crew cut hair.

Turning, he faced Patrick. "This car is just terrific, Mr. Owens."

Patrick looked pleased. He was hoping his visitor would want the car.

Marty fought back the urge to ask how the car came to be all apart. Especially when he remembered what simply mentioning the Roadster had done to Patrick. He decided it prudent to let well enough alone, for now. After all, the car wasn't his. Yet.

"Do you know if all the parts are here? he asked.

"I'm confident you'll find nothing missing," he was assured.

"Do you have a price in mind, Mr. Owens?"

"Let's go back to the house and talk about it," Patrick said.

After carefully recovering the Roadster's body, Marty stepped back for one more look at the scattered treasure-trove of Roadster parts.

Seated in the living room, he could hear his new acquaintances discussing something in the kitchen. Time to concentrate on the upcoming pricing discussion. These were nice people and he already liked them. For that reason, he couldn't bring himself to haggle over the price. He intended to go all out to possess this jewel of a car.

But what if the car wasn't assembled to the point of being ready to travel in the time remaining? What then? he wondered. Maybe he should get their agreement that he could return, in the summer, to finish the reassembly.

"So, Marty," Patrick began, "how much is a car like that worth, nowadays?"

"I have no idea, Mr. Owens. I've never seen one in that condition. The ones I've looked into, before coming here, were selling for just under a thousand dollars. Your car is in a whole other class."

"I see," Patrick said.

"I can offer you two thousand dollars."

No one on the other side of the bargaining table spoke. Worse, he was dismayed to see Mary looking over at Patrick, while slowly shaking her head. Patrick didn't look like he was going to jump at his offer either.

This was chilling. He didn't expect this reaction. How he had misjudged these people. Damn, they could buy a brand new car with two grand, he reasoned.

"Twenty-two hundred! That's all I've got with me, except for traveling money."

Patrick had that same troubled expression on his face.

"You don't understand. The only reason I asked about the Roadster's value is because we don't want to overcharge you. Mary reminded me that we paid about six-hundred dollars for the car. So, that's our asking price, six-hundred dollars."

Marty's brain was rattling. This has to be a dream. None of it made any sense. Old cars aren't valued this way. Clearly, they didn't understand their bargaining position. He began to slowly shake his head.

"No, that isn't fair. It's very good of you, but it's not fair. You could get much more for it. I can't leave here, thinking I've swindled you. I can't."

Patrick frowned. "Look, young fella, the money isn't the foremost issue from our point of view. And don't forget, you still have to assemble that car to take it home."

No reaction, so Patrick continued.

"First and foremost is the Roadster's new owner. We've listened to you go on about Roadsters and I watched you out there in the garage. We believe you'll love our son's car, as he did. He would want you to have his car. That's what matters most to us."

Mary spoke up. "I've been after Patrick to sell that car for years. It isn't right to let Bennie's car waste away like that. And today, for the first time, he agrees. It seems you've come along at just the right time."

After some difficult haggling, Marty got the price up to a thousand dollars.

Patrick put his foot down and said, "Okay then, one thousand dollars, take it or leave it, young man."

The two men went to the auto club and got a bill of sale made out. Ten travelers checks changed hands.

Marty, at last, had his Roadster. And the best day of his life still had many hours left.

On the return trip, Patrick suggested that Marty might want to park his trailer alongside the garage until he left for home. It was the first thing he did that afternoon.

For the balance of the day he poked around in the garage and formulated an assembly process in his mind. The reassembly presented a number of problems that were certain to prove difficult to solve. The majority he could handle by himself. A few he could not. Most daunting, was how he was going to lift the body onto the frame by himself.

As the afternoon turned into evening, he was still at it. At one point, he glanced outside and noticed it was dark already. Damn, it was late! He placed the little booklet into his pocket.

The Roadster's five wheels, tires still mounted, were stacked along the side wall.

Removing one, he rolled it outside and set it in the back of the station wagon. Soon all five were loaded.

He closed the rear of the Nomad and turned back to the garage for one last look at the treasure site.

Closing up, he quietly drove off into the night in search of food and shelter.

# 6

At the top of the agenda, the next morning was the need to locate new tires for the Roadster. The existing tires were now twenty-five years old and, although they looked serviceable, there was no way he would risk using them.

After calling around, a tire store claimed to have just what he wanted. It took some searching, but eventually the tires were located. They'd been in stock for years, but were wrapped in tape and the whitewalls looked great. He bought five and to finalize the deal, the store manager threw in new inner-tubes, free mounting and balancing.

With the new tires installed on the wheels, several men rolled them outside and loaded them into the Chevy.

Leaving the tire store, he stopped at an auto parts store armed with a lengthy list of needs.

Yesterday, while locating and examining car parts in the garage, he decided to make the Roadster ready, in all respects, for the road.

His plan was to drive his folks around Carlisle as soon as he had backed the Roadster off the trailer. Through their years of support, they'd earned it. Besides, he was sure they'd get a big kick out of it.

His tentative schedule called for an early Monday departure. Today being Wednesday, that allowed four days to complete the assembly. Sunday could be used, if necessary, but for now that day was set aside for a little sightseeing.

Much of this optimism was spawned by a discovery last evening. The engine was not rusted and he could rotate its internals by hand. This was extremely good news.

This morning, he'd come up with a solution for the body lift. Recruit gas station attendants to lend a hand, about five of the largest. He'd make it worth their while.

Driving back to the Owens without the trailer was a treat. He got there just before ten o'clock and turned into the driveway. Slowly rolling past the Owens' kitchen door, he was startled to find the garage doors open on the Roadster's side.

The Nomad's door flew open and his left leg was out the door before the car came to a stop. He hurried inside, but saw no one. Then a head popped up in the back of the garage.

"Take one step closer and I'll scream," the young woman warned.

"My name's Gibson, the new owner—"

"What the hell's wrong with you? Don't you know enough to knock? You scared the life out of me," she said.

She looked to be in her mid-twenties. Pretty nice looking but, damn, what a disposition! he thought.

"Who the hell are you, anyway? And what're you doing... How did you get in here?" His voice boomed with authority.

"Go to hell!" she shot back.

Just then Mary appeared in the driveway.

"Oh, I see you two have met," she said with a smile on her face. "Catherine, I'm afraid I've run out of sweeper bags."

Pushing her way out of the garage, Catherine replied, "I'll go and get some."

She walked past Marty without a look or word and went into the Owens' kitchen. He turned to Mary with a smile.

"Well, at least she didn't take a poke at me."

"This is all my fault, Marty. It seemed a good time to come out here and clean this place while you were gone. It's positively filthy. I had no idea. Catherine asked if she could help. She's our house guest."

At that moment, Catherine came out of the house, got into her Corvair convertible and drove off.

"Is Catherine your granddaughter, Mary?"

"No, but for many years she's been as close to being one as we could have hoped. She was born and raised in that house," Mary said pointing to the house next door. "Over the years, we saw a great deal of her. She was such a delightful girl."

Marty found that hard to believe and his face must have showed it.

"Oh, believe me, Marty, this isn't the same girl. Once she went off to college, we rarely saw her. "The poor thing has had more than her share of troubles. When she was barely ten, she'd lost her mother to polio. Catherine was very brave, but the loss had to be devastating, they'd been so close."

"And, her father, is he still..."

"Oh, yes, John is a wonderful man. He's a pilot with the airlines and lives in San Francisco. Once Catherine left for college, his company moved him back to overseas flights. He told me he wanted her to come up and stay with him, or he'd see to it she had a nice place to live nearby. He worries about her so."

"But, being with you and Patrick has to be the next best thing."

"Catherine's only been here for the past few weeks. Patrick and I thought it was going to be like old times. So many nights she stayed with us when John was late getting home. He was flying from Los Angeles to San Francisco and back, in those days.

"But, now, it's different. You saw how she is. It's that horrible man..."

Mary paused, looked around and apologized for keeping him from his work before returning to the house.

Marty was busy moving furniture out of the garage when Catherine returned. He stopped what he was doing as she came up to him.

"I'm so sorry about my behavior earlier. It was very rude of me," she said.

"I was a pompous jerk," Marty replied.

"You must think I'm some kind of crazy person. I'm so embarrassed."

"Forget it." He smiled and rubbed his hand on his pant leg before he held it out and introduced himself.

She took his hand and smiled. "Cathy McCann. "We were cleaning in there, but there's so much... We filled two sweeper bags in no time. If it's okay with you, I'd like to get back to work."

"Yes, sure. And thanks for the help, Cathy.

"I'll have this furniture out of here, just as soon as I can. Patrick told me he'd intended to throw it out, but never got around to it. I volunteered to haul it away."

"Don't do anything with it for an hour or so," she said. "I've called some antique dealers and one of them will be here soon."

The dealer offered sixty dollars for the lot and the deal was struck. As soon as the truck had rolled out of the driveway, Cathy said, "I've got to get ready for work. With an early start tomorrow, I can finish up in there."

Marty turned to his task, dragging the heavy frame across the canvas he'd placed on the floor and setting it down midway out the door. The reassembly had begun.

Having just set the four heavy blocks of wood near their needed locations, he was about to lift the front end of the frame when he turned and saw Patrick headed his way.

"Can I help with anything?"

"Your timing couldn't be better, Patrick. I need to get the frame up onto these blocks."

He then lifted the front end of the frame several feet off the ground, while Patrick slid the blocks of wood into position. After repeating the process at the other end, the frame was at an ideal height for reassembly.

"I'll be back soon," Patrick said as he headed for his like-new '56 Packard and backed it out of the garage. Marty watched as Cathy came out of the house, got into the Packard and they drove off.

Both the front and rear axles and the associated components were laying on the floor, in place, under the frame, when he heard the Packard returning. Patrick parked the car and came over.

Marty asked, "Is there anything wrong with Cathy's Corvair, Patrick? Maybe I could—"

"No, it's fine." Patrick replied quietly.

"Did I say something wrong?"

Patrick looked away, shaking his head. "Several years ago, Cathy was attacked by a man. He went to prison for attempted rape, but he's recently been released. Now, she believes he's after her again, the dirty swine. Please excuse me, son, but I get so..."

"So now you drive her to work and go for her at night?"

"Yes. She still works at the airport, where the trouble happened. He caught her in the parking lot, coming out of work one night. It's not going to happen again, not if I can help it."

"Did she notify the police?"

"We wanted her to, but she doesn't want to cause any more trouble. And she's not absolutely certain about his following her.

"She was such a different girl before that filth happened," Patrick said. "I'm sorry, Marty. I never meant to burden you."

"No, I'm glad you told me, Patrick. I won't be around that long, but maybe I could help a little. Why not let me drive her to and from work? It would give you a little break."

"That's very good of you, Marty, but—"

"Patrick, back home, I'm a cop. Cathy would be safe with me."

"I'll ask her," the older man said and then smiled. He patted Marty on the shoulder and left.

Marty closed up the garage that evening, close to eleven o'clock. It had been a productive day. The bare frame was now a rolling chassis. It had axles, wheels, springs, brakes and steering. The reassembly was off to a great start.

# 7

Marty sat in the diner, waiting for his breakfast to arrive. His first responsibility of the day was to tend to the Nomad's damaged fender and bumper. He'd let his enthusiasm for the Roadster run roughshod over common sense.

He had been stopped by the police last night because of the damaged fender. The headlight pointing at the ground had brought the unwanted attention and the end of the bumper pointing ahead like a spear didn't help matters.

After checking out Marty's license and the car's registration, the officer had said, "This is your lucky night, fella. You won't be getting a citation."

"Thank you, officer."

"However, if we should chance to meet again under similar circumstances, visitor or not, tsk, tsk, tsk. Understand?"

"Yes, sir, I do," Marty had said, embarrassed.

After breakfast he called around to wrecking yards and easily found what he needed. Unloading the parts in front of the garage, he set to work installing them on the Nomad. He only stopped work once when Cathy came out to invite him to come inside for lunch.

The finished job on the Nomad was a big improvement, if one overlooked the fact that the replacement fender was a darker blue than the rest of the light blue and white car. That would be dealt with once he was back home.

All set to drive Cathy to work, he strolled over and opened the garage door to look over his progress on the Roadster. He discovered that Cathy had finished cleaning the garage. What an improvement!

After dropping her off at the airport terminal, Marty stopped at an equipment rental store. Back at the garage, he rolled the chassis out into the bright sun and mid-seventy degree temperatures. Damn, it looks impressive, he thought, walking around to admire it from all sides. It still lacked shock absorbers and the brake activating hookup, but that would come.

Yesterday, he'd found the Roadster's license plates, dated 1941. It thrilled him that this was the first time in twenty years that part of the Roadster had been outdoors. Another milestone for the Project!

He removed the rented engine hoist from the back of his Nomad in sections and assembled it. It was on wheels and he rolled the hoist inside the garage and hooked the engine to it. In no time, the engine was outside. A few minutes later and the transmission was outside as well. He found the cans that contained the fasteners, and in short order the engine and transmission were bolted together, dangling in the air above the chassis.

As the heavy components were carefully lowered into place, he marveled at the ease with which the car was coming together. It was almost too easy. Aside from a little dust, all that was needed was to locate the part, then the can containing the correct fasteners, tighten some bolts and, presto.

Besides the assembly work, it was necessary to grease the wheel bearings and such, but that, too, was a breeze. He was having the time of his life. With the engine and transmission permanently installed on the now much heavier chassis, he rolled the whole works back inside the garage and locked up.

After returning the hoist to the rental store and enjoying a good meal, he returned to the garage and the chassis work continued. The brakes were finished and adjusted and the shocks were now in place, as well the gas tank and fuel line. It was close to ten o'clock when he shut down assembly operations.

After a quick shower and change of clothes, he set out for the airport.

Even prior to entering the freeway, he had the feeling he was being followed. There was a car, either the fifth or sixth behind, that caught his attention. It was easy to spot since it had one headlight much dimmer than the other. To confirm his suspicion, he pulled out to pass a few cars and then returned to the right lane. Sure enough, the other car did the same to maintain its trailing position.

He remembered a car leaving the motel parking area soon after his departure, but couldn't recall the dim headlight. Before that, an hour or so before he left the garage, he thought someone or something passed by, just outside the open garage doors. He had gone outside to investigate, but found nothing amiss.

Who would be following me? he wondered. I hardly know anyone out here.

Signaling his exit, he went down the off ramp. Midway along, he pulled over and stopped, to watch for the mystery car to come along.

"There it is, a forty-nine DeSoto four door sedan," he mumbled.

He had to wait for nearly a dozen cars to pass before he could get underway. Time enough for the DeSoto to vanish. The notion he was being followed brought a smile.

At the airport parking lot, he had to settle for a fairly distant place to park. A quick check of the time and he set out for the terminal. There was no need to hurry.

On the way to the airport that afternoon, Marty had suggested that she let him help her get over some of her fears of being followed. At first, she seemed upset that Patrick had confided in him, but she realized he had done so out of concern for her safety. She was hesitant about Marty's suggestion, but had agreed to try. The first step was for her to walk to the car rather than being picked up at the terminal door.

As the two left the terminal, Marty explained, "Once you're back to driving yourself to work, you'll want to park randomly. If you park in the same general area, that could make it easier for a guy who's up to no good."

Cathy nodded.

"Also, you'll want to park in a well lit area. Wait until you see others walking in your direction and stick closely to them for as long as you can. And wear good running shoes, just in case. Oh, and here's another thing, you—"

Suddenly Cathy grabbed Marty's arm and muttered, "It's him!"

There was a man sitting on the front fender of his Nomad.

"Okay, Cath, go back to the terminal right now."

She turned back and Marty approached the man. So this was the scum who'd tried to rape Cathy.

"Do I know you, fella?" Marty asked.

"Duke."

"Well, Duke, I don't appreciate my car being used for a park bench, so how about getting off?"

Duke sneered, glancing in Cathy's direction.

"Three seconds, buddy, then I'll help you off," Marty said pleasantly with a smile.

"Don't get excited, buddy," Duke said with a smirk. He slid off the fender and headed for Cathy, who was standing nearby.

Rushing to catch up, Marty reached out and grabbed his arm.

"Just a minute," Marty said. Looking at Cathy, he asked, "You want to talk to this guy?"

"No!" she said firmly.

"You heard the lady. Now back off."

"Take a hike, tough guy," came the mocking reply.

"Come on, Cathy," Marty said, as he led her to the Nomad and opened the passenger door. "Lock the door," he whispered.

Duke blocked the way as Marty came around the car. He took a swing, but the punch glanced off Marty's shoulder. And a second later Marty was behind his adversary, locking up his arm, forcing Duke to his knees, and then flat on his stomach—a perfect position to be handcuffed.

Now in complete control, Marty said in a low voice, "How long you stay down there is up to you."

Duke struggled to free himself but soon settled down.

"It's not right, you scaring that girl," Marty said.

"The hell with you!" came the reply. "It's none of your damned business!"

"I'd say you made it my business. Keep up with this crap and watch how fast I get your parole officer interested in you. Hell, maybe I can convince him you don't belong out here with civilians."

Marty stood up and backed off a few steps.

"What're you, a cop?" Duke asked, now on his feet.

"That's right."

"Yeah, well, I saw your plates. You're no cop around here. Around here, you're nothing, man."

Marty glared back at the man, realizing he had been drinking.

"Let me tell you somethin', cop," Duke said, pulling a match from his jacket pocket. Duke flicked his thumb and held the lighted match at eye level, whispering, "I know where your garage is."

Marty swatted the match out of his adversary's hand. Duke took another swing at him, but lost his balance this time, and hit the pavement hard.

"What the hell's wrong with you? You in a big hurry to get back to your prison pals?" Marty raised his voice this time.

Cathy jumped out of the car, and before Marty could stop her, she kicked Duke in the head.

"Son of a bitch! you damn near put my eye out," Duke groaned as he got up and backed away. "This ain't over, tough guy." He turned and slinked off among the parked cars.

On the way home, Marty and Cathy stopped for coffee. As Marty finished off his apple pie and pushed the dish aside, he said, "I know some ways for you to defend yourself, if you're interested, Cathy. It wouldn't take much time, maybe a half-hour each morning."

Cathy nodded, but said nothing.

"Oh, how's your foot?"

She cringed. "It's pretty sore."

"Too sore to go dancing Saturday night?"

"Are you asking me out on a date?"

"I owe you for the great job you did in the garage."

Cathy smiled.

"Look, Cath, maybe it would do you good to get out with people. We're not all jerks, like that guy, Duke."

"It's a wonderful idea. You're right, it has been a while."

On their way home, Marty was feeling pretty good. Maybe tonight, after seeing Duke down on the ground, flopping around helplessly, Cathy might sleep a little easier.

He saw her to the door, then moved on to the garage. He'd taken the arson threat very seriously. So much so, he decided to work on the Roadster until dawn, or as close to it as possible.

Submerged in silence, he began to think about Cathy and that nut, Duke. Something wasn't right. He felt it in his gut.

Cathy sat on her bed thinking about Duke. Everyone blamed him for her change in personality, assuming the attempted rape had traumatized her. Such was not the case. Despite her attempts to fend off the memories, her mind went back to her freshman year of college.

It was just prior to Christmas break and several dozen college friends gathered to celebrate at a fellow student's home. His parents were in Europe and the house was wide open, with no need to worry about adult interference. The punch was spiked, although Cathy hadn't realized it. Unaccustomed to alcohol, it wasn't long before she was staggering drunk, swept away by the party atmosphere. She passed out on the couch, as the party swirled around her.

She woke up early the next morning, disoriented and fuzzyheaded. Stumbling over her fallen comrades, she located her purse and made her way to the front door. She started her car, and sat there a moment trying to clear her head, determined to go back to her dorm room and crawl into bed.

She drove around the unfamiliar residential streets. Nothing registered and she realized she was lost. As she squinted in concentration, trying to find something she recognized, a young boy came out of the cars parked along the curb. A silent scream filled her throat. She stumbled from the car and stared at the boy sprawled on the street, his bicycle badly bent and folded newspapers scattered around. The boy's foot was twisted at an impossible angle. A large dog suddenly appeared and ran over to lick the boy's face. As Cathy moved toward the pair, the dog growled, then charged toward her. She ran to her car and slammed the door shut behind her, as the enraged dog clawed at the convertible top.

Terrified, in shock, still half drunk, Cathy looked around. There were no lights in any of the nearby houses. The boy needed immediate medical attention, but her mind betrayed her. Get away from here! Just drive away! Jail! Prison! Scandal! Without pause, the words were repeated, drowning out her ability to think. Neither tears nor holding her hands over her ears helped.

Overwhelmed, she gave in and drove off down the street, frantically hoping to find a phone. It seemed to take forever, but she finally saw a service station.

"Please, I need to use your phone," she gasped, as she ran inside the station.

The young attendant gave her the once over and shrugged. "Sure, it's over there on the desk."

"I want to report an accident," she yelled into the phone.

"Okay, calm down, lady," the voice at the other end of the line said. "Where's the accident?"

"Where?"

"Right. Where's the accident? What's the address?"

"I ...I ..." Cathy hung up the phone and returned to her car, trembling. She slowly retraced her route, searching for the intersection that would take her back to the accident. A police car raced by. An ambulance followed, lights flashing. Cathy watched them pass, then turned her car in the opposite direction and fled.

The newspaper featured the hit and run story on the front page the following morning. Cathy stared at the picture of the boy in the street. According to the article, he'd been diagnosed with a badly damaged leg and other injuries. She threw the paper down when she reached the statement about the possible need for an amputation.

Cathy became obsessed with the idea that the police were searching for her at that very moment. She recoiled at the thought of returning to classes, or to any of the places she normally frequented.

She directed her fury at God. He'd turned his back on her. Again. He'd taken her mother, despite all the prayers, promises, begging, weeping and pleas, that no ten year old girl should be left without a mom. Now, he'd led her to this, harming a helpless child. With unshakable conviction, she believed God had singled her out and was determined to cloud her life for the rest of her days.

Her belief made it easier to heap the numbing guilt on the newsboy. He shouldn't have been darting out from between cars. He should have been wearing bright clothes. None of her rationales counteracted the contempt she felt for herself.

She dropped out of college and withdrew from the world she'd known and her friends and acquaintances, afraid she would somehow let slip her foul deed. Too often the hatred she harbored for herself spilled out onto people around her and she wanted others to suffer, just as she suffered.

Shaking off his somber thoughts, Marty got out of the car. After removing the padlock from the door, he hauled the four heavy pieces of wood he used to support the frame over to the entrance and stacked them so the garage doors couldn't be closed easily.

His idea was to slow down the closing of the doors while he was inside. Being trapped with the Roadster in a fire was something that could be avoided through precautions.

It was just after four in the morning, when he began to close up for the night. The chassis was checked and double checked and the exhaust system was in place and connected to the engine. He could think of nothing that had been missed. The body was now ready to join the rolling chassis.

After some sleep he would return to work on the engine and get it running.

# 8

The alarm went off at ten A.M. and soon after Marty headed out the door. He'd barely removed the key from the motel door, when he groaned, "Aw, for ..."

A brick was embedded in the Nomad's windshield. He walked around the car, to make sure nothing else was damaged.

"Duke!" He removed the brick, got into the car and drove off. Getting out in the parking lot of Chastaine's Police Department, he hustled inside, carrying the brick. When he asked about filing a vandalism report, he was sent to see a Detective Jones.

Two desks were placed so the two detectives were facing each other.

"Detective Jones?"

Two voices responded.

"You're both Jones? Related?"

The older man snorted. "Not a chance! What can we do for you?"

"My car was vandalized." He held up the brick. "This turned the windshield into a nameless roadmap during the night."

"Got some identification?" the younger Jones asked, motioning to the empty chair.

Marty handed over his state police ID card.

"You're a cop?" the younger Jones asked, reaching across the desk to hand the ID to his partner.

Marty smiled. "God help me, yes." He turned to the older Jones. "You know, back home, once a person gets to know me, it usually takes them a month, or more, before they start throwing stuff at my car. I've been out here less than a week."

Neither cop smiled or commented.

"I believe I know who did this." He gave them a brief description of Cathy's situation.

"You guys get to take vacation in January?" the younger Jones asked.

"I'm between assignments, using the time to do some treasure hunting."

The detectives exchanged glances.

"The thing is, I've got the guy's license plate number and his name. Maybe you could extend some professional courtesy and let me in on his criminal background. Last night, this guy harassed Cathy, the girl I was with, and he warned that our confrontation wasn't over, so it would be helpful to know what I'm up against."

"Where can you be reached?" the older Jones asked.

He wrote down Marty's motel number and the Owens' address.

The cops recommended a place to get the windshield replaced. The job took less than an hour and he was at the garage just after lunch.

Soon after he arrived, Cathy came out to the garage carrying a cup of coffee and a small radio.

"Hell's bells, I nearly forgot! You ready to start?" he asked.

"Ready."

"Just so we're clear on this, I don't know how to show you a way to beat the bejeepers out of this guy, just how to escape from him. Okay?"

"Yes, I understand."

She explained how he came up to her from behind and what he did.

"Like this?" he asked, placing his left arm under her chin.

"Yes, that's it."

He released his grip and came around to face her. Then he showed her how an elbow was a weapon. After demonstrating how to get more power into her elbow swing by setting her feet for better balance and swiveling her upper body, they moved on to other measures.

Next came head butting the enemy's nose, then stomping on his toenails and more. Later, they moved to a frontal attack, featuring the most devastating tactic of all—a kick between the legs.

Most of the moves were practiced in slow motion. Other options were merely discussed. Like raking the eyes with her fingernails and screaming.

"Nothing will bring people to your aid faster than a woman's blood curdling scream," he said.

Running the gamut of possibilities took forty-five minutes, but Cathy made no complaint.

"You did good, Cath. Tomorrow, we'll practice what we covered today. If either of us comes up with other ideas, we'll include them. Okay?"

She gave him a hug and went into the house.

It was a little after one o'clock, when he rolled the chassis outside. The rest of the day would be spent on getting the engine ready to run.

Fully engrossed in his work, he didn't notice Patrick, until he stopped next to the chassis.

"Looks like you're making wonderful progress, Marty."

"The papers in those cans are so specific everything is practically falling together," he replied.

He explained what he was doing with the engine.

"The reason I came out here was to apologize for your difficulty last night. Cathy told us about it."

"No need to apologize, Patrick. I'd hoped he might cross the line, give a reason for some jail time, but he was careful not to oblige."

"There is one other thing, Son, you're working some very late hours."

"I'm sorry, Patrick, I tried to keep the noise down."

"Oh, good Lord, it's not that. I know how important this car is to you, but so is sleep."

Marty frowned and looked away. Then he told Patrick about the garage threat.

"He'd have to be out of his mind to try anything in daylight. I don't think he's crazy. So, if he tries to make good on his threat, it'll be at night, probably after everyone is in bed. I'm really sorry about this, Patrick."

Patrick put his hand on Marty's shoulder and shook his head. "It's not your fault."

"You should probably know the rest," Marty said. Going to his car, he returned with the brick. "You need to see this, Patrick." As the two men walked to the side of the garage, Marty said, "I made this discovery a little earlier." Stopping, he knelt down and inserted the brick into the garage wall.

"Why that arrogant... He's showing us that he can come and go as he pleases!" Patrick said. His jaws tightened. "I insist on paying for your windshield, Marty."

"Thanks, Patrick, it's good of you, but it's none of your doing. Besides, I filed a police report that I'll send in to my insurance company when I get home."

Patrick looked up at the outside light fixtures above the garage doors, while saying, "They haven't worked for some time. I intended to change the bulbs, that's probably what's wrong with them."

He went into the garage and called out, "Marty, would you get the ladder?"

In minutes Marty replaced the bulbs and both men smiled. In addition, Patrick located a second garden hose, which now allowed coverage of the entire garage.

"We'll leave the downstairs house lights on all night. Hopefully, he'll think we're watching for him. How late do you plan to work tonight?"

"Until daylight, if I can."

"I'll take over about two, so you can get some sleep," Patrick said, "There's a wonderful view of the garage from our room and a phone. No arguments, young fella."

"Thanks, Patrick."

"By the way, Marty, we're indebted to you for the self-defense course you're teaching Catherine and for taking her dancing on Saturday night. It's good medicine. So are you."

He patted Marty on the shoulder several times and turned to leave. "Oh, I almost forgot, Son. You're invited to dinner. We're having a roast tonight and Mary is a chef-quality cook. About six. You can wash up when you come in. I'll call you, when it's time."

Throughout his life, Marty had always relished the approval of his parents. Now he basked in those same feelings as he watched this kindly man walk along the driveway.

Later in the afternoon, after taking Cathy to work, he was busy replacing the front and top components of the engine. They'd been removed for the purpose of lubrication and the replacement of possibly dried out gaskets. The starter motor, generator and carburetor were checked out as well. Tonight, the carburetor would be getting a new gasket set and the distributor was scheduled for new points and condenser.

It would soon be time to get out and recruit gas station attendants for tomorrow's body lift. First, he needed to place another can under the engine to drain the remaining oil.

At that moment, the older Detective Jones walked up the driveway. He was a big man, big boned, as the saying goes. At about six feet, three inches tall, and probably weighing in at around two hundred and twenty-five pounds, he was quite a specimen. There was no trace of a gut on this guy.

Marty liked the other Jones better. The younger Jones seemed more people friendly. This Jones struck him as a bit gruff and kind of cold. Maybe his years on the force were responsible. Marty wondered if a similar fate awaited him.

"So, this is where you're holed up," Jones said.

"Detective Jones, welcome."

"It's Sam to you, Marty. What's all this?" he said, looking over the chassis.

"Trying to collect my treasure, so I can go home."

"Where's the rest of it?"

"Inside."

The two men went into the garage out of the bright sun and Sam began to look around as his eyes adjusted.

"What the hell happened?"

"Beats me. This is how I found it, except for a ton of dust."

Sam frowned. "I stopped at the house and the fella said I'd find you out here. Damned if I don't remember him. I couldn't have been more than sixteen when I came here to buy this car. Hell, I had visions of a Roadster dancin' in my pea brain. One look from that guy and I knew I was sunk."

"I know what you mean. I got that same look at first."

Sam got the fifty cent tour. The highlight for him came when the two men pulled back the covering on the Roadster's body.

"Good Lord, would you look at this!" Sam said. "Hot damn! With this car I could have had every female in my high school after my fat ass."

Then he turned and looked at Marty. "How come he sold the Roadster to you? What're you, family?"

Marty shrugged. "No. His wife said I came along at the right time."

Sam was turning out to be an easy guy to like.

"I've been nutty about cars since I was a kid. I've got a real nice '34 Ford three window coupe. Owned it since I got out of the Navy," Sam said.

"Wish you'd brought it with you."

"So, this is how far along you are, huh?"

"Yeah, the engine is almost ready to fire up."

"How you figure on getting that body lifted on?"

Without waiting for an answer, Sam said, "I could round up about four guys, plus you and me. That should about do it, don't you think?"

"Sam, that'd put you right up there with Robin Roberts and Johnny Unitas, in my book."

"Oh, the reason I came by was to let you know about my visit to see your buddy, this morning. Looked like he got hit by a large truck. He gave me a bunch of bullshit about falling down two flights of stairs last night. How the hell does anybody fall down two flights of stairs?"

Marty looked him in the eye. "Just between us, Sam?"

Sam nodded. Then the beginning of a grin appeared.

"He went down the first flight after trying to deck me. And the second flight after indicating how he's going to burn down this garage before trying to clip me again. I jerked him around some, but I didn't smack him. He'd been drinking, probably had a snoot full."

"I'd have thrown him out a damned window."

Both men chuckled.

Sam said, "Anyway, I warned him how we'd be making tracks for his rock, if anybody even farts near Cathy. Don't think it did much good, though."

"I appreciate it."

"His parole officer is off this afternoon. I'll hook up with him Monday and fill him in on this jerk. Jarvis is a no nonsense kind of guy, old school, you know? If anyone can get through to him, Jarvis can."

"Thanks again."

"Just between you and me, this guy is a zero. We've got nothing on him, except for that Cathy thing. I think he's all mouth."

Marty smiled and patted his visitor on the shoulder.

"Just to be on the safe side, I'll get the neighborhood patrols to keep a close watch on this place, especially the night guys."

Marty was grateful. The look on his face showed it.

Sam smiled. "Sorry that weasel is screwin' up your treasurin', buddy."

The two men slowly walked out the driveway.

"There's something else," Sam said, hesitantly. "I've come up with something you need to file away. It's about Cathy."

Marty's brow wrinkled.

"Did you know she's had this trouble before?"

"No, I didn't."

"Some young guy, about her age, got pulled in on her say so. He got the choice of jail or a stint in the military. Apparently, there were no witnesses that time around. He joined the Army. He's out now, so I called him, without identifying myself. Soon as I mentioned her name, he slammed up on me. Damn near broke my eardrum."

The two exchanged concerned glances.

"Take my advice, Marty. Watch your ass."

This was more professional courtesy than Marty had anticipated.

When they reached Sam's car, he said, "I'll have my buddies here about ten in the morning."

Darkness moved in soon after he returned to the garage. He had by then removed the two large cans of oil that had drained from the engine's crankcase and carefully placed them on the floor inside the Nomad. Changing the Roadster's oil reminded him that the Nomad's oil also needed changing.

He rolled the chassis into the garage and after locking up drove off to the nearest service station to dispose of the twenty year old oil.

Patrick was right. Mary was a chef-quality cook. Marty had scarfed up two helpings of everything before returning to his work in the garage. Later on, Mary was all smiles, when she told Patrick she hadn't seen an appetite like that in a very long time.

Out at the garage, Marty switched on the outside lights, snatched the padlock from the door and moved the heavy wood into position between the doors. Hoisting the large gas can, he poured the dollar's worth into the Roadster's tank, saving a small amount in a soup can for later to prime the engine.

The quiet evening hours were a very productive time. He completed a tedious carburetor rebuild and installed the vital engine parts including new fan belts and fuel pump before installing the spark plug wires. Hurrying to finish up the engine, he set the radiator in place, hooked up its four hoses and filled the cooling system. After installing the battery cables, he checked his watch.

It was time to go for Cathy. He left the outside garage lights on and smiled at their effectiveness.

When they stopped for coffee and a snack, Marty thought about how Cathy had gone from negative to positive so quickly.

"I asked about a good place to go dancing," Cathy said, interrupting his thought.

"And," he said.

"There's this wonderful place about five miles from us. I was told we wouldn't be disappointed."

"Good work, Cath."

Cathy looked around the diner then leaned over the table and in a near whisper said, "To tell the truth, I'm getting a little nervous. It's been quite a while."

Marty smiled. "Don't expect too much, Cath. I'm no Gene Kelly."

Back at the garage, he spent the rest of his night lining up the cans and checking their contents, all seventeen of them. An impressive number of empties had accumulated under the shelves. He sorted and stacked them, after setting aside two as souvenirs.

By the time two A.M. came, the lights were on upstairs and he waved to Patrick.

# 9

Cathy was first up on Marty's agenda the following morning for her lesson on self-defense training. After she left, Marty wandered around inside the garage looking things over. With the chassis outside it was downright spacious. He was trying to select the best places to grip the body to lift it onto the chassis when he heard the sound of car engines.

Five old cars poured through the driveway and came to rest on both sides of the garage. He recognized Sam, the cop, in a '34 Ford coupe. It was a beauty, as were the others. He waved to the younger Jones, in a '40 Ford coupe.

Sam introduced everyone. All five were cops. Two were highway patrol officers and the others were Chastaine's finest.

"All of us live in or around Chastaine," Sam said. "We like to get together like this, run our cars and help each other out."

Marty was caught up in the excitement. Soon he was wandering around, checking out each of the cars. Besides the two early Fords, there was a '41 Plymouth convertible with a Chevy engine, a '40 Buick convertible and a '49 Mercury coupe.

He learned how long each of the men had owned their cars, how they came to acquire them and the shape they were in when they changed hands. Standard old-car owner talk.

When it was his turn, he told them about his years of searching and his treasure hunting experiences since arriving here in this Roadster haven. His new friends seemed impressed. They were even more impressed when he and Sam rolled back the Roadster's body covering.

There was complete silence for a few moments, as they crowded around for a closer look.

"What'd I tell you?" Sam bragged to his friends.

Now everyone was talking, awed by the Roadster's condition after all these years, awed by its odometer reading of twelve thousand miles.

"You hit the jackpot!" one of the group called out.

"Want to sell it?" another asked, laughing.

"Look, I've turned green," said another.

"You're one lucky bastard, Marty," said the younger Jones.

For this group, times like this didn't come any better.

Then they got down to the business at hand. Off came their rings and watches and everyone had made sure to wear a shirt without buttons or anything that might possibly mar the beautiful paint.

Sam and Marty went outside and rolled the chassis to the waiting body.

"Okay, let's lift on three. One–two–three!" Sam called out.

"Watch out for fingers and toes, fellas, here we come," Marty cautioned. He watched carefully as the chassis glided into position. "Okay, fellas, let her down." This moment was critical as the body slowly dropped over a foot, then to within an inch of touching, and then, when he eased the chassis forward a little, the body made contact.

"Great job, everybody!" Marty called out.

Marty and the younger Jones each took a side and bolted the body down while the others stood by looking over the finished product.

"I live for this shit," one of them said.

Marty then went around, shaking hands and thanking each one for their help.

"What about the fenders and all? Want some help with that stuff?" one of the men asked.

"I'd really appreciate it, fellas."

The garage turned into a beehive of activity. They paired off and spread out. Marty and Sam began by installing the windshield assembly. Others worked on the grille and front fenders and bumper, while another team tended to the car's rear area.

Next, Sam helped Marty install the folding convertible top assembly and then came the doors. On went the running boards and finally the hubcaps.

The garage fell silent as the men circled the Roadster, admiring their work.

"These past few hours were as close to a miracle as I'll ever get," Marty said, in a voice filled with emotion.

"I'll probably bore the living shit out of my wife telling her about all this," said another.

Marty walked over to Sam and said, "Fellas, how am I ever going to repay you?

"You already paid us, buddy. This is the best time I've had in quite a while," Sam said.

The others quickly agreed.

The younger Jones came up to Marty and draped an arm over his shoulder. Look, buddy, if it bothers you that much, I know a donut shop with the best coffee in town, and you can buy."

That brought a unanimous response and it was settled.

At the coffee shop, the six men pulled a couple of tables together and kept the waitress busy. These guys reminded Marty of his car buddies back home and he felt like one of the gang. Everyone joined in with "Remember the time you—" stories. And Marty settled back and laughed along with the others. What a perfect day!

Talk then turned to the drag races.

"Marty, are you going to Pomona tomorrow?"

Marty looked puzzled.

"The Winternationals!" the same man said. "It's the first time for anything this big. Drag racers from all over the country are gonna be here."

"Oh yeah, I guess I did hear about it. Is it too late to get a ticket?"

"I've got an extra one," another in the group said. "You're welcome to go with us."

It was getting late, as they left the donut shop and Marty was anxious to get back to gawk at his trophy.

Back at the garage, Marty spent more time admiring the car than he intended. He gently stroked a length of its classic body. Sixteen years of dreams, searching, and now this, he was thinking. And, in a week or so, his course in life might be taking a new direction.

Time to go. Reluctantly, he turned on the outside garage lights and locked up. His cop buddies were right. He was a lucky bastard.

Marty returned to the Owens' home right on time.

"Catherine will be right down," Mary said.

Marty felt tonight was sort of a coming out event for Cathy and he was determined to make it memorable. Cathy did her part.

"You look like a million, Cath," Marty said as she came down the stairs.

The first few hours of the evening went by quickly. They told each other about themselves and sometimes the conversation revealed a minor secret or two. He told her a few silly jokes and teased her.

This is a whole new Marty, Cathy thought. This is their first time together when he isn't all business. He's easy to be around, and fun.

They left the dance floor when their dinner arrived.

"Patrick told me you're a police officer, Marty."

"Yeah, for almost a year."

"Why a police officer?"

Marty smiled. "It's a long story, Cath. It's all Trooper Kendrick's fault," he began. "I was just a little squirt when Trooper Kendrick came into my life. He and his wife moved into our neighborhood, a few houses down the street from us. A few days later, I saw him pull into his driveway wearing this really neat looking hat and he was in uniform. So, I went over and started up a conversation with him."

"And you were just a little squirt, did you say?" she asked, with a smile.

"No one ever accused me of being shy. A pest? Sure, I got that a lot," he laughed. "I eventually got around to asking if he was a forest ranger. He explained that he was a police officer and they were called state troopers. He told me all about what they do and that their number one job was to save lives. I was fascinated. He became my hero."

Cathy smiled as he talked.

Marty continued. "In time, they added a third member to their family. Not long after, the Kendricks moved away."

"And, so you wanted to become a state trooper, too," Cathy said.

"Oh, I don't know. He probably influenced me, but how much or how little I can't say. How do you quantify that kind of thing, Cath?" He looked off toward the dance floor. "One thing though, what he said about saving lives was pretty powerful stuff to a pesky kid."

She smiled and nodded.

Looking a little embarrassed, he said, "Hey, we're letting a lot of good music go to waste."

At least fifty or sixty couples were maneuvering for floor space.

"Are you having a good time, Cath?" he asked.

"Oh, yes. I've certainly been missing out on a lot of wonderful times."

In a few minutes Marty mentioned the guys who'd helped him and his plans to join them the next day at the drag races. Cathy face clouded and her tone took on a sharper edge for a while, but Marty didn't seem to notice the change in mood.

The band was a seven piece group and now they played one of Cathy's all time favorites.

Just as the song ended, she whispered in his ear, "I love you, Marty."

He pulled back, unsure of what she said.

"I said, I love you," she repeated.

He searched her eyes and they were saying the same thing.

"Did you hear what I said?" Her voice had grown shrill.

He pulled her closer. "Cathy, tonight's just two friends out for a nice time. I think you're very special, too, but I have to leave for home Monday."

He could feel her body grow rigid. His mind raced to find something he might say to soften his words. "Cathy, what you said means a lot to me."

She was scowling.

"Cath, I'm sorry I didn't mention this before, but there's someone back home. Margie. Next week, I'm going to ask her to marry me."

She kicked him in the groin and violently pushed him away.

As he slumped to the floor she screamed, "You lousy bastard!"

All eyes turned their way as Marty curled up on the floor in pain. His eyes were glassy.

Cathy spun around and pushed her way through the crowd. Moments later she returned and tried to kick him in the head. Several men caught her in time and shoved her away.

She jerked free and ran to the ladies' room and locked herself inside a stall. "Oh, Mommy!" she moaned. Tears poured down her face as she fell against the partition.

The crying stopped abruptly. "Who am I? I don't know anymore. Is this cruelty ever going to end?" she asked in a strange voice. "Apparently not! I was so sure it was ending when Marty arrived. Finally a guy who treated me with kindness. Who looked out for me. Who cared whether I lived or died. Who changed my life. Who took me dancing. Who spit in my face!"

She paused, breathing heavily, a twisted smile on her face. "So, I'm just supposed to forget this? Let bygones be bygones? That's it? Oh, no! Not so fast, buster! You're in my world now. Welcome to hell, you deceitful bastard!"

Suddenly her hand shot out and bashed the toilet paper roll from its holder.

When Marty could finally focus somewhat, he found himself sitting at a table. Several men hovered over him, asking if they could help.

Then two police officers found him. They got little to nothing from him, other than his repeated mumbling that he would be okay in a few more minutes.

"I just got a little out of line," he told them. "Everything is okay. No, I don't want to see a doctor."

The officers left after speaking with several other dancers who described what little they'd seen.

What happened? he wondered. Where is she? What brought on such violent behavior? He looked around the room.

The door to the ladies restroom opened and Cathy appeared, her make-up smeared, her eyes red and puffy.

Marty stood up and slowly walked toward her.

"Cathy, we have time, if you want to tidy up a little."

Without a word, she turned and went back inside.

As he waited, another woman entered the restroom but quickly came out, and charged off, looking for someone.

Moments later, Cathy came out of the ladies' room and walked toward the front door, Marty quietly following.

"Don't you leave here!" a man shouted, hurrying into the restroom.

Two police officers intercepted them as they stepped outside. "Over here, please," one of them said.

Just then a man burst through the front door.

"I want her arrested! I want her arrested, now!"

Marty stepped in front of Cathy. "Who the hell are you?"

"I own this place," the man shouted, "and she's destroyed the ladies' room!" He turned to the officers. "You should see it! Broken mirrors, a sink pulled from the wall, a commode turned over, water everywhere!"

One of the officers went inside just as a second car had arrived with two more cops.

Marty listened in disbelief as the owner ticked off the damages. Cathy stared off, making no attempt to deny anything he said.

Meanwhile, the other officer came back outside and nodded to the owner. "It's pretty bad in there."

Over Marty's protests, they handcuffed Cathy and put her in the back of the squad car. He watched her face but she showed no fear, no remorse, only indifference.

He called Patrick and Mary and told them what had happened. Patrick arrived at the police station and took the owner aside, offering to pay all damages. They reached an understanding and the owner dropped the charges. Within the hour, Cathy was released.

Marty followed Patrick and Cathy back to the house. Cathy had gone upstairs without a word to anyone. Mary had followed.

The two men sat down at the kitchen table and Marty told Patrick what had happened.

"She's leaving." Mary said, coming into the kitchen.

"When?" Patrick asked, frowning.

"Tonight. I tried to talk her out of it, begged her not to go."

The words were no sooner out of her mouth when Cathy came downstairs with her suitcases. She paused for a moment and glared at Marty, her eyes full of hatred.

Then she turned and went out the door.

"I thought I was helping," Marty said. "I thought taking her out for a good time would help her get more comfortable around other people, around men."

"It's none of your doing," Mary assured him.

"It's not you ..."

Patrick was interrupted by the sounds of an engine racing, squealing tires, followed by a very loud crash. Marty scrambled outside, with Patrick and Mary not far behind.

Cathy's Corvair was embedded in the Roadster's side of the garage. The doors had taken the brunt of the collision and half the door was pushed inside the garage a bit. Its upper hinge had been torn loose and the heavy door sagged inward at the top. Marty was outraged.

Cathy was slumped over the steering wheel unconscious.

The front end of her car was badly damaged, but the engine was still running. Marty forced the door open and turned off the ignition.

"Call an ambulance," Marty called to the stunned couple.

"I'll take care of it," Patrick said, heading for the house.

"Cathy," Marty said quietly. She slowly responded and he kept her quiet and still, until the ambulance arrived.

The police showed up as well. Marty told the officers that the Corvair's gas pedal had been sticking. He was pretty sure the officers didn't buy his fairy tale, but since Patrick made no complaint, they completed their report and left.

After the ambulance left with Cathy, Marty drove Mary and Patrick to the hospital. Afraid his anger might show, he said little.

The doctor said, "I didn't find anything other than the bump on her head. If there are no complications, I expect she'll be released in the next twenty-four hours."

# 10

It was just past four in the morning, when Marty dropped off the Owens. He pulled up to the garage and parked behind the Corvair. He checked on the garage door and it looked as if the top had sagged in a bit more. He just stood there for a few moments shaking his head in disbelief.

In the quiet, his thoughts shifted to Cathy. As he saw it, he'd acted like a big brother. He'd protected her from Duke, not only for her sake but for the Owens' peace of mind. So, in only four days, how the hell could things get from that to this mess? What could he have said or done to make Cathy believe he had a romantic interest in her?

And what about Mary and Patrick? What must they be thinking?

How could a day, so good, turn out so bad? he wondered. All things considered, this had turned into one helluva trip.

No drag races for me today, he decided. At the designated time, Marty met his friends and begged off the event. They understood.

Back at his motel room, he took a shower and tried to get some sleep. No dice. His imagination was working overtime. Finally, he got dressed and went looking for a place to get some breakfast. Afterwards, he felt a little better. Time to face the music.

Marty stood in the driveway, looking at the two burned rubber trails leading to the Corvair's resting place. The trick was to pry the car away from the doors without their toppling. Unable to think of a way to support the garage door from the outside, he shifted the transmission into neutral and gripping the back bumper, tried to pull it free. Nothing doing.

He slowly paced around, hands on hips, puffing heavily. While he caught his breath, he began to look at the bright side of this mess. The Corvair was a lightweight, as cars go, with its engine and most of its weight in the rear. Under the hood was the trunk comprised of little more than sheet metal. As he saw it, ramming the Corvair into the garage, head first, made as much sense as whacking a ball with the wrong end of a club or bat.

Out of options, he got into the Corvair and turned the ignition key. It started! After a deep breath, he attempted to shift into reverse. Grinding gears could be heard all over the neighborhood. He cringed.

Ever so carefully, he tried to shift into first gear and it worked! Then he slowly moved the gearshift into reverse and it silently engaged. After another deep breath, he slowly let the clutch out. The car vibrated slightly and then stalled. Rubbing his hands together nervously, some of those feelings from last week returned. The ones during that hairy ride down the icy mountain.

Putting that out of his mind, he restarted the engine and revved it gently a few times. When he let out the clutch this time, the car rolled back about five feet.

There was a large gap at the bottom of the garage doors and, after removing his jacket, he slipped inside to find the Roadster still flawless!

"Marty, are you in there?" Patrick called out.

Marty quickly crawled back out and stood up, brushing himself off.

"Hope all is well in there, Son. We're off to church."

"The Roadster is fine. So far, so good. Thanks for asking."

"Did you sleep in there all night?"

"No, I've been here a little while. I had to look in on the Roadster, to be sure it was okay," he said with a smile.

"This afternoon I'll get in touch with some workmen we've dealt with occasionally. I'll ask them to come over as soon as possible."

"Have you heard how Cathy's doing?" he asked

"I've already called this morning and she's fine, Marty. They may release her later today," Mary replied.

He smiled and nodded but, regarding her release, he was thinking, damn!

After discussing it with Mary, he was able to reach inside the luggage compartment for Cathy's bags and set them just inside the kitchen door.

Afterwards he went back inside the garage and collected the Roadster's upholstery for both the passenger and rumble seat compartments. He'd picked up a bottle of leather treatment at a sporting goods store the other day and he set to work.

The leather looked perfect, but it wasn't very pliable. This oil worked on stiff baseball gloves and he was counting on it doing the same for the seat and door panels. The first application was literally sucked up, but after the second time around, the suppleness began to return. Tomorrow he would take a chance on sitting on the seat.

By early afternoon, he had wrapped up work on the car's interior. Just as he was about to crawl out of the garage, he remembered the license plates and installed them. The 1941 plates looked good on the Roadster, like they belonged.

Before leaving, he parked the Corvair parallel to the garage doors. It made a pretty decent barricade. After locking her car, he placed the keys on top of its rear tire, out of sight.

There was a lot on his mind as he left the garage. He drove around for a while and ended up at the ocean. Off came his shoes and socks and, minutes later, he was walking ankle deep with the surf lapping over his feet. The water was cold, but not cold enough for him to get out. He wandered aimlessly. The warm sun and balmy temperatures gave him a sense of peace.

Eventually his problems pushed their way to the forefront. His original plan had been to leave for home tomorrow. Right now, it didn't look very promising. There was still much to do.

After talking with his cop friends at the donut shop yesterday, he'd decided to wrap the car for its trip home. They recommended a surplus parachute from the local Army-Navy outlet as a good first layer of protection. In addition, tomorrow he'd get a water repellent tarp from the hardware store plus several lengths of clothes-line to tie everything down.

The covering would keep prying eyes from his treasure. Equally important, it would make the unveiling of his sparkler in front of his folks all the more impressive.

He formulated the remaining steps in his mind. First, he needed to get the engine running. It should also get a good washing. And, the trailer had to be hitched to the Nomad, so the car could be loaded, then wrapped.

Having walked so far that his Chevy was out of sight, he turned back and his thoughts returned to tomorrow. All that preparation was going to take time. How much time? Assuming the car was available by ten or eleven in the morning, and everything went smoothly, it would be mid-afternoon, at best, before he could be ready to travel. Shaking his head, he muttered, "No good."

If there was going to be a problem with either the Nomad or the trailer and its load, it would likely show up during the first tank full of gas. That would include a few hours of darkness by his calculations. Trouble during daylight hours was bad enough. Trouble at night, when repair shops had closed, might leave him stranded in the middle of nowhere.

Maybe it would be better to wait until Tuesday and get an early start, he reasoned. That would mean an extra night of sentry duty. Damn! He'd just wait and see how things panned out tomorrow. It wasn't necessary to decide now.

His thoughts shifted to Cathy and Duke. By far, his greatest concern centered around the Roadster. Through some kind of twisted logic, Cathy seemed to have fixated on the Roadster as the ideal way to hurt him. So he wondered, if I was her, how would I go about destroying a car? And would she try again? In any case, if and when she, or Duke, came, it would most likely be after bedtime and after he had returned to the motel.

On the way back to Chastaine, he stopped off to eat and then went directly to the motel and hit the sack.

By eight o'clock that evening, Marty was on the way over to the Owens' garage. After parking behind the house, he turned on the outside garage lights and stared at the sagging door, while shaking his head and making "Um, um, um" sounds.

Tonight he'd brought along the blanket from his motel bed. In order to listen for intruders, he kept the windows rolled down a few inches. By midnight, he wished he had an additional blanket.

Later on he heard footsteps, and quietly got out of the car ready to pounce.

But it was a cop! Both men were surprised.

"You Marty?" the cop asked in a whisper.

"Yeah, glad to meet you ..."

"Jeb."

The two men moved out of the light.

"Sam asked us to keep a close watch on the garage." Noticing the Corvair and the sagging door, Jeb said, "He didn't mention that white bulldozer."

"I really appreciate your looking out for me, Jeb."

"How late you figure on staying out here?"

"I hope to be relieved by two," he answered, motioning to the house.

"Wish we could do more than stop by once an hour, but that's the best we can do."

"That's plenty. Thanks."

After Jeb left, he wrapped himself in the blanket and got back into the car.

# 11

The next morning after a few hours sleep, Marty shopped for the materials he would need to wrap the Roadster. He made one other stop at a radio repair shop for a new speaker for the car.

It was just after nine when he pulled up behind the Corvair. Not a sign of the workmen for the garage door. So much for an early start on the Roadster.

Not knowing what else to do, he opened the Nomad's tailgate and pulled out the parachute. Tediously, he cut the strings from the silk and discarded the rest. Looking at the time, he grabbed the new radio speaker and squirmed inside the garage. Yesterday, he'd discovered the car's radio didn't work. After removing it from the dash, the only obvious thing wrong was that the speaker had deteriorated to the point where, just touching the paper cone caused pieces to crumble and fall away.

With the replacement in place, he switched on the ignition key and the radio. There was only a loud buzzing noise. The car probably needed to be outside the garage for decent reception, he reasoned.

"Beautiful," he said, after installing the side curtains. Now she's ready for that bath, he thought, smiling to himself.

Just as he crawled out of the garage, he saw the rear portion of an old DeSoto pass out of sight.

"Duke!" He ran out to the street and watched as the car stopped for the stop sign and turned left. "Damn it! It was him!" he grumbled. He ran back to the Chevy. Before long he was at the stop sign turning left, just as Duke had done.

Marty cruised an area of six or seven square blocks looking for the old DeSoto, trying to push aside the idea of what Duke was doing around here. It was obvious. But he couldn't be thinking of starting a fire in broad daylight. Duke couldn't be that dumb.

Finding no sign of the DeSoto, he drove to the local gas station for a fill-up. On the way, he braked hard enough to squeal the tires. "I'll be damned!" he muttered. "There it is!" The DeSoto was parked in front of a small restaurant.

He parked the Chevy out of sight and returned on foot. After finding a good location, to watch the comings and goings, he waited. Fifteen minutes passed and he was growing impatient. He decided to just confront Duke.

But Marty froze when he reached to open the restaurant door. Duke was sitting at a table with Cathy. "Dammit!" he said, stepping away from the entrance. What the hell's going on here?

They didn't look especially affectionate toward each other, but they didn't seem hostile either. It looked like they were planning something or maybe comparing notes. Whatever they were doing, he didn't like it. And what was that she'd passed to Duke? Money?

Having seen enough, he moved out of sight. While he waited he chastised himself for being so stupid. Until the dance he'd felt compassion for her. To what end? More trouble than he could have imagined. And the wasted time. Time that could have been spent on the Roadster. What a fool.

The next time the restaurant door opened, the two of them came out. Marty had already made up his mind to follow Cathy. He wanted to know what she was up to or, at the very least, where she was staying.

The two split up and Cathy headed for the business district in a car Marty had never seen. She pulled into a parking lot and entered a hardware store. Marty pulled into an alley and returned on foot to watch for her.

She came out of the store carrying a bag. It looked heavy. She put the bag in her car, crossed the street and started walking, with Marty following at a safe distance. She stopped at a movie theater ticket booth and went inside.

He went to the theater and checked the movie's running time. He'd return before one o'clock.

On the way to his car, he stopped to check out Cathy's vehicle. It was a rental, according to the metal license plate frame. The two door Ford Falcon was white, like her Corvair, but not quite so bright. Going to the driver's door, he spotted what she had gotten in the hardware store—what looked like a hammer, screwdriver and hatchet. His pulse quickened and his skin crawled.

There they were on display, her weapons of choice. You had to have a hammer, if your intended victim was a car. And a good, sturdy, flat blade screwdriver to keep your other hand busy gouging paint. But what the hell did she need that hatchet for? "It must be for me," he whispered.

He went into the hardware store and bought a padlock, a good one, since Cathy had a key to the existing lock.

No matter what it took, he'd be leaving California no later than tomorrow. The Roadster was too close to going home to take unnecessary risks.

It was a little past noon, when he returned to the Owens' garage. Patrick came out and called him for lunch.

"Good news, Marty. Catherine's out of the hospital," Mary said.

He smiled and nodded. "That's great!"

"She stopped by late yesterday afternoon and picked up her bags," she added.

"She left for San Francisco on a midnight flight," Patrick said.

Marty didn't comment.

The phone rang and Mary went into another room to answer it.

"I certainly hope the change of scene will do some good," Patrick said, trying to sound positive.

Minutes later, Mary came back to the kitchen, all smiles. "That was Catherine, calling from San Francisco. She wanted to apologize for all the trouble she'd caused. She's going to be staying with her father until things sort themselves out. She said she would take care of the Corvair later if that was okay with us, which it is."

Marty checked his watch, thinking San Francisco my ass! It must have been a crummy movie. He thought about correcting Cathy's deceit but before he could decide, the repairmen drove along the driveway and passed by the kitchen.

Their late arrival made it official. It would be too late to set out for home today.

The men looked over the situation, both inside and out.

"That's quite a car in there," the boss said to Marty.

"It is so far," Marty said, in a voice filled with concern.

Both men assured him his car was in no danger. Marty volunteered to be the inside man, when it came time to remove the door.

Inside, he went to his toolbox and removed the breaker bar. It was a heavy, long handled, practically unbreakable steel bar used to break loose extremely tight, rusted or stubborn nuts and bolts. At nearly a foot and one-half in length, it was a suitable defense against a hammer or hatchet. From now on, it would be kept close at hand.

Marty helped lower the damaged door to the ground.

"This reminds me of the doors on our firehouse back home," he told his co-workers.

The men helped push the Roadster outside and along the driveway, out of harm's way.

Shortly after, the Roadster's engine belched a spreading cloud of dark and bluish smoke from its tailpipe for several seconds. After stalling a few times, he had the small V8 engine running. He hovered over it, making adjustments until he was satisfied, while alternately checking for leaks underneath. Not once did the smile of satisfaction leave his face.

Afterwards, he got in and drove the car to the end of the driveway and backed up to his starting point a number of times. Back under the car he went to adjust a brake that was dragging a little. After another test run, he parked the car over behind the house under a large shade tree.

Blocking the driveway with the Nomad, to prevent another ramming attempt, it was time to wash the old car.

The Roadster sparkled like a flawless gem when he had wiped it dry. From any angle, the view was postcard quality. He set about waxing the paint and chrome.

Patrick was back at the garage, settling up with the repairmen, while they prepared to leave.

After the men left, Patrick joined Marty for a close-up look at the old car. They slowly circled the car several times and Marty urged Patrick to get in. Patrick slid onto the seat and ran his hands around the steering wheel.

"Go ahead and start it up," Marty said.

"It's amazing, Marty. You've turned the clock back for me." He looked toward the house and then the yard. "Little's changed. Even this car is just the way I remembered it."

Looking straight ahead, he said, "I bought this car for Mary's birthday. She was thrilled. So was our son, Ben. Much more than either of us realized at the time.

"In those days, my work took me out of town a great deal. Eventually, I hooked on with a local company, Lockheed Aircraft, which allowed me to return home permanently. But those long separations did damage. Ben and I had grown apart to the point where he no longer called me, Dad. I focused on becoming his father again. This car turned out to be a shortcut to him, I'm certain of it."

"How so?"

"Ben was carrying a big torch for the Roadster. In that regard, and some others, you remind me of him."

Marty smiled. "What kind of work did you do, Patrick?"

"I was an electrical engineer. Oh, and how did the Roadster help ... I shamelessly used it to win him over. At every opportunity, when he was around, I'd take this car to run errands. His eyes absolutely lit up when I invited him along. What unforgettable memories!"

Patrick looked off into the distance at things only he could see.

"Mary no longer used this car much, once I was home. We talked it over and decided to keep it for Ben. She reminded me that selling it would have broken his heart and he was nearing driving age."

"What a lucky guy."

"For his sixteenth birthday, his present from us came in a little box, containing the Roadster's keys. I wish you could have seen his face."

Marty smiled. "I know how I would have reacted."

"You must think I'm a maudlin old man, young fella."

"I'm thinking how alike you and my dad seem."

"Ben didn't go to college, as we'd hoped. Instead, he took a job at a filling station, not far from here. He began to get speeding citations for racing from traffic light to traffic light." Patrick snapped his fingers, trying to remember the term.

"Drag racing?"

"Yes, that's it. He collected one citation too many, as is turned out. Ben was devastated when his driving license was suspended for an entire year. Our biggest concern was that youthful impetuousness might lead him to sneak the Roadster out some night. It was quite a dilemma."

Marty was nodding his head, sensing that the bad stuff was moments away.

"After weighing a very short list of options, none of which involved selling his car, I asked him to join me for a walk one late summer evening.

"I put it to him that he could make good use of the next twelve months. Why not disassemble his car and make any repairs or changes to it that he wished? Then, by the time his license was reinstated, the car would be in tip-top condition. In addition, he would know the car inside and out. I presented the idea as a wonderful, once in a lifetime opportunity. The dividing wall and those shelving units were incentives.

"By Thanksgiving, the car was close to the way you found it."

"Ben made the reassembly very easy for me."

Patrick nodded, but then his jaw muscles began twitching and he looked angry. "Then came Pearl Harbor. A few months later, he joined the Air Corps. And, as they say, that was that."

"The Depression and then the war. Your generation sure had it rough."

"Yes, I suppose we did." He became silent for a moment. "After the war, my trips out to his workshop became less frequent. Ben had asked me to take care of his car until he returned. I did. It's just that it was obvious Ben would never return, except possibly in spirit.

"I'll make you a promise, Patrick. If Ben's spirit comes around in the coming years to see how his Roadster is faring, he'll leave with a smile on his face."

Patrick smiled and bumped Marty's arm. "I knew that the day we met, son. We knew you were the one meant to have this car."

Patrick picked up the envelope he'd placed on the Roadster's roof when he got into the car.

"Mary did some digging and found a few things she hoped you might want," he said, handing the envelope to Marty. "I think you'll find this interesting."

After Patrick had gone back to the house, Marty opened the envelope and pulled out the Roadster's owner's manual and, among various other papers, its sales invoice. Marty was elated. The total cost of the Roadster had been $614.15. To a car guy, this document was as important as his birth certificate, maybe more so. What a find, Marty thought.

He put the envelope into the Roadster's glove box on top of the ownership papers. His eyes turned to the radio and he also switched on the ignition. It took a few seconds for the old tubes to warm up, but after tweaking the dial a little, Connie Francis was screaming, "Everybody's Somebody's Fool." He adjusted the volume and listened with a smile and then a wave of nostalgia came over him. What'd you expect? he asked himself, the Andrews Sisters to be wailing "Boogie Woogie Bugle Boy," or some 1940s song? What was the last song to come out of this old Philco back then? he wondered.

At that moment, a distinguished looking, well-dressed man, probably in his mid-fifties, came up the driveway. Marty turned off the radio.

Spotting the Roadster, the stranger pointed toward the car and asked, "May I?"

Marty smiled and motioned for the man to join him.

"Good Heavens!" the man said as he walked around the Roadster. "Oh, sorry, I'm J.C. Williams. My friends call me J.C. I heard about your car and had to come see for myself. The description sounded too good to be true. I can see that, if anything, they shortchanged this sweetheart."

The two men spent some time talking about the assembly of the car and its remarkable condition.

"Twelve thousand miles? That's it?"

Marty nodded. Then he opened the glove box and handed J.C. the sales invoice.

"You even have documentation!" Shaking his head, he said, "This has to be the find of the century! I've got a nice little collection of Ford Roadsters, starting with a thirty-two and ending with a forty-two convertible. Thirteen in all. Ever see three thirty-six Roadsters, side by side?"

Marty's jaw dropped.

"Why not come over this evening and take a look for yourself?"

"Ordinarily I'd jump at an offer like that, J.C., but I'm leaving for home tomorrow."

"I see. You want to get an early start, do you? No problem. Come over early, say about six. We'll throw a couple of steaks on the grill, have a drink and you'll still be home early."

"Could you give me a couple of minutes?"

"Certainly."

Marty knocked on the kitchen door and told Patrick about the invitation.

"Go ahead and enjoy yourself. Don't worry. I'll keep a close watch, while you're gone."

"I'll be back not later than eight. And thank you, my friend."

Returning to J.C., Marty said, "You're on! And thanks for the invitation."

"Good, good. Where are you staying? I'll send a car. I'm kind of off the beaten path. Might be hard to find in the dark. Don't want you to get lost and waste time. Let me know when you want to get home and I'll see to it."

After J.C. left Marty stood smiling in the driveway. Had he left for home this morning, what a missed golden opportunity, he thought.

With the Roadster safely tucked away, he turned on the outside lights and moved the Corvair in front of the garage doors. On the way to his motel, his thoughts turned to J.C. He was already convinced J.C. must be the best financially fixed guy he'd ever met.

Unknown to Marty, J.C. was indeed wealthy. He'd made his fortune in real estate, presently owning the two largest office buildings in the city among other widely held financial interests. A self-made millionaire many times over, his journey through the Depression era was one of deprivation. He'd scrimped and saved the proceeds of the two jobs he held simultaneously, putting everything into his investments. There was nothing available to spend on the Ford Roadsters he so admired throughout the thirties.

With those times now only a memory, he'd turned to collecting at least one Ford Roadster from each of those years. Testaments of his struggles, sacrifices and ultimate triumph.

At 5:40 the car arrived at the motel and whisked Marty away. Soon the Lincoln slowed for the tall iron gates to open. Snaking uphill, Marty noticed the small lights on each side of the driveway. Suddenly a large house loomed in the darkness. Not far away was a long and rectangular shaped building. When the car stopped Marty stepped out, taking in a magnificent view below. All of Chastaine was on display.

J.C. was a gracious host and Marty felt at home in his spacious and beautiful home. Time passed quickly and, after an excellent meal, J.C. led the way to the car show.

"I'll be damned," Marty said as he looked over the old cars.

"Every one of them is the best example in existence that I'm aware of," J.C. boasted.

The building was impressive. Immaculately cared for, the floor was tiled and the walls covered with knotty pine. He took a deep breath. Yep, the unmistakable aroma of old cars. Best of all, the place was huge.

It would easily accommodate another dozen cars. Marty could think of nowhere on earth he'd rather be at this moment.

As they walked around the various cars, J.C. gave a brief history of each. It was now time for the main event. J.C. opened a door to an adjoining, smaller room. Switching on the lights, he turned to Marty.

"I've saved the best for last, my all-time favorite Roadsters."

There they were, just as J.C. had said. One was tan, another maroon and the third was black, Marty's favorite Roadster color. The sight of them together like this overwhelmed him.

"My God!" he said, in a whisper.

"Do you have a favorite, young man?"

Marty walked around each car, saving the black one for last. Without taking his eyes off of this vision of automotive glory, he shook his head. "It would be tougher than picking one puppy out of a litter," he finally answered.

"The reason I asked," J.C. said, "is because I'd like to put a proposition to you. I'd like to trade Roadsters." J.C. motioned to the trio. "Any one of those, for yours."

Marty smiled, but shook his head.

"And," J.C. said, noticing Marty's reticence, "any brand new car of your choosing. I'm a silent partner in many of the car dealerships around here. If it's not in stock, they'll order it. A red Thunderbird with a big engine, and you can go down the order form and check off every option that's available. Or, maybe a highly optioned Corvette. Whichever you choose, it will be delivered to your door in Pennsylvania."

J.C. couldn't read Marty's expressionless face.

"Or," J.C. continued, "any one of these, plus five thousand dollars. Do the deal, Marty," he urged, "and I'll have the cash in your hands, inside five minutes."

"I need a few minutes," Marty replied.

"Certainly. Of course," J. C. said with a smile as he went back into the other room.

Marty's head was spinning. There was no way I would get a deal like this from anyone else, he thought. Not during this or the next decade.

Sure, an original car like his was extremely rare and more valuable than any of the cars he was being offered, but not by five thousand dollars! Not even close, he reasoned.

Only a week ago, he would have given his right arm for any one of these cars J.C. was offering. He could go home with this black beauty and far more money than he had before coming out here! It could be an even bigger down payment for a house! He could see Margie's smiling face. That did it!

He turned to join his host, but his mind had already shifted gears and now something was wrong. No longer was he thinking about J.C.'s offers. Now, all sorts of thoughts flooded his mind. He recalled all those disappointing, fruitless trips to locate his Roadster over the years. About how the Heavens opened up twelve days ago, sending him all the way across the country, to the end of his rainbow.

And then there was the joy of bringing the Roadster back to life. Making its life part of his. The things he'd planned during the past week, the things they would do together over his lifetime.

And what did J.C. have in mind for his car? Maybe going on a short drive once or twice a year to keep its vitals lubricated? Then back to the darkness of its tomb?

"We believe you'll love our son's car, as he did." Wasn't that what Patrick said? Hell, that's why they sold the car to me, for crying out loud. What could he tell them? That he unloaded it for a big profit? They could have done that! How could he look them in the eye?

J.C. was surprised by Marty's decision. He did little to hide his disappointment, though it didn't stop him from raising his offer a few more times. Then, still desperate to put over this deal, he began to describe the perils of transporting the Roadster on such an unstable platform.

"Don't forget, Marty, you may well run into rain, ice and snow, once you leave California. Not to mention traffic accidents. Accept my offer and the car will be delivered to your door in Pennsylvania in an enclosed truck."

Marty smiled, while shaking his head. "Sorry, J.C."

J.C. slowly and grudgingly came around to accept Marty's decision and they parted with a handshake as J.C. called for his driver to take Marty back to the motel.

J.C. had little experience with disappointment. During his early days of empire building, he took great pride in all his accomplishments. Later on, once his success was no longer in doubt, he changed. The only joy he got out of a new acquisition was when it was the best. Nothing illustrated his penchant better than his two office buildings. The one he bought first was magnificent, but it was four stories less than the tallest in town. For the first time, it gnawed at him. Over the next five years, he obsessed over the one building he coveted. Its owner disliked J.C. and refused to sell. But later, after the owner died, J.C. acquired the building from the heirs.

From that point on, only the best became J.C.'s criteria for making an acquisition.

Then came the idea of his car collection. Sometimes the best available was not very impressive. J.C. allowed that a car could be acquired and restored to its former glory, so long as there was nothing better available.

After Marty left, J.C. stood at a large window in his house watching the lights of the Lincoln move down the hill. After it was out of sight, he picked up the telephone. He wasn't finished yet.

"Charlie, it's J.C. The kid just left. No, he won't sell. Yeah, it did appear to be vacuum sealed all these years. Hell, yes, he knows what he's got. He gave me a lot of sentimental bullshit about not selling."

"So, what do you want to do?"

"Aw, dammit! Charlie, I hate to ask this, but I need your help again. I've got to have that car. There's not another like it. It'd be the centerpiece of my collection."

"I understand, J.C. No problem."

"I'll be very grateful, understand?"

"Of course. We won't let you down. I'll call Morg right away and get ready. When's he pullin' out?"

"Early tomorrow," J.C. replied.

"Well, he's got to be taking Route 66, so I think we'll leave before light and wait for him to come along."

"Good. Good." J.C. gave him the particulars on the Nomad and the trailer. "He's alone, so check the motels," J.C. advised.

"Yeah, he's got to sleep sometime."

"Charlie, you guys be very careful. Don't take unnecessary chances. Listen, if anything goes bad, I'll take care of you guys. You know that, don't you?"

"J.C., it's me, remember?"

"And for God sakes, be careful with the Roadster. No high speed chases and I don't want anyone getting hurt, either. This is to be one of your straight repossession-like jobs, right?"

"That's the plan, J.C. How far should we go?"

"Use your best judgment, that's all I ask."

J.C. softly set the receiver down onto the cradle, then picked up a half-full bottle of wine and flung it across the room. "Son of a bitch," he shouted.

Charlie and Morgan were highly skilled men. J.C. felt fortunate to have them in his employ. At a dinner meeting one evening, years ago, the owner of a new car dealership casually mentioned an unusual problem with an employee.

"We hired this guy for our body and paint shop about a month ago, and now I've got to let him go," the owner said.

"So," J.C. said, "some people just aren't cut out—"

"No, it's nothing like that. His work is outstanding, but he's so slow he's not earning his keep."

"Is he good enough to work on my old cars?"

"You bet he is, that's why I mentioned him."

Over the next week, J.C. got to see some of Morg's work. J.C. offered him a job, restoring his planned acquisition of Ford Roadsters. Already, the first two cars were awaiting his magic touch.

J.C. also needed a really top-notch mechanic and Morg knew

such a man. He brought Charlie around and J.C. hired him on the spot.

Charlie was crazy about auto racing. He was sought out by various race teams needing a chief mechanic. But racing was seasonal and paid little to those who didn't reach the winner's circle. Rather than spending the off-season working in an auto repair shop, Charlie chose instead to repossess cars for the local banks, on a commission basis. He jumped at the chance to take over J.C.'s planned car collection.

With Charlie in the fold, J.C. had his artists, and Charlie found an employer who paid well and had no problem with his summer absences.

J.C. set them up in a garage with all the necessities.

One afternoon, about halfway along with his growing Roadster collection, J.C. stopped by the shop. He'd just made a generous offer on a well worn, '36 Ford Roadster. In spite of his considerable bargaining skills, J.C. failed to close the deal. Pacing around the shop, he grumbled, "This one could have been the centerpiece of my collection."

The two employees listened sympathetically for a while, before Charlie posed a remedy.

"Suppose we can repossess that car and get you perfectly legal ownership papers?"

J.C. at first thought Charlie was joking. "Absolutely not. You fellas steal things?"

"Actually, we don't think of it as stealing. We retrieve things that become lost. There's little risk for us and zero for you," Morg said.

"You've been good to us, boss, so we're just offerin' an option is all," Charlie said.

Nowadays, J.C.'s display contained two counterfeits. The Black '32 and the aforementioned maroon '36 Roadster. It was rare that J.C. allowed anyone to see his collection. Even so, the owners of the '32 and '36 would never make the connection between their worn out cars and the dazzlers they'd become.

Marty was relaxed on his way back to the motel. He had made a very important decision and now he was without a trace of regret. He smiled thinking about this evening. His car buddies back home would thrill to the story of J.C. and his collection of Fords.

His thoughts turned to guard duty tonight. He had only to ward off those two screwballs just this one, last night. Tomorrow, he and the Roadster were going home!

He returned to the Owens' garage, to watch for any hint of danger, but it was very quiet. By eleven-thirty, he was fighting sleep. He sat up at the sound of footsteps and hustled to the driveway with the breaking bar in hand.

"Marty, it's the cops," Jeb said. "You okay? Looks like you could use some sleep, buddy."

"Not yet. But thanks for taking time to look in on me."

"See you on our next rotation in about an hour."

Less than an hour later, Jeb was back again, carrying coffee and a bag containing a few donuts.

"I really appreciate this," Marty said.

"How long you gonna stay tonight?"

Marty looked upstairs. "Until my relief shows at two o'clock."

# 12

After an uneventful night and adequate sleep, Marty drove to the Owens' garage for the last time. The day he'd been waiting for had arrived.

Like other mornings in California, it was nippy during the early hours. After several turns around the Roadster, admiring its beauty, Marty made ready for his departure.

He hooked the trailer to the Nomad. After checking their tire pressures with the trailer in tow and placed perfectly, Marty started the Roadster and slowly drove it to the trailer and on the second try, the car was in place.

After attaching hold-down chains to the Roadster's axles, he gripped the rear bumper, and tried rocking the car back and forth. It was secure. He went into the garage to collect his souvenir cans and his long and heavy toolbox. Now there was no longer a trace of the Roadster in the garage.

Mary and Patrick soon joined him as he began to wrap the Roadster. The work went quickly and well. After taking one last look around he went inside to have coffee with the Owens. He decided not to mention seeing Cathy.

During their good-byes, Marty said, "You've been very good to me, like family." Shrugging his shoulders, he added, "There's no way I can repay your kindness. Please know I'll never forget either of you."

"Call us when you get home, Marty. We'll worry about you until then." Mary said.

"Best of luck, young fella. You'll always be welcome here," Patrick added.

After hugging them both, Marty slowly pulled out. Freeway traffic was heavy as usual. He joined the flow and stayed put in his lane across greater Los Angeles.

A glance in the rearview mirror at the Roadster had him grinning. Sure, there was the unpleasantness of Cathy and Duke but what counted most went extremely well. In another four days, he could close the Roadster Project. Mission accomplished!

The Chevy was humming along just fine and the gas tank was half-full. He considered stopping at San Bernardino for gas, but the needle had moved little by then. Barstow was up ahead and a good place to judge the Chevy's gas consumption.

There it was, Cajon Pass. He remembered it well. This was going to be the ultimate test of the Nomad's pulling power. If the Chevy could make this climb, it could get over anything else he'd face on the way home.

The Chevy needed to climb thousands of feet in a very few miles. Fortunately, there were two lanes of traffic in both directions. Approaching the base of Cajon Pass, he was doing sixty miles an hour and the trailer wasn't a problem. But ever so slowly the Nomad was giving up its speed to the steep grade. When the speedometer dropped to fifty, he shifted to a lower gear.

Nearly half-way to the top, the temperature gage reached three-quarters. This was something that had never happened. But then, the Chevy hadn't been pulling the extra weight.

His body tensed as the speedometer dropped to forty-five miles an hour. The engine was working hard, but holding its own.

There it was. Finally. The high desert. A few miles beyond that agonizing grind the Chevy's engine temperature returned to normal. Climbing Cajon was a big confidence builder.

What a terrific car this is, he thought.

On the way to Barstow, Marty's mind began to wander. He revisited other trips he'd made with the Chevy and trailer. He was reliving the visit to Michigan, during the summer of 1959.

"What the hell?" he said, leaning forward, straining to make out what was on the side of the highway up ahead. "Oh, no!" he groaned, slapping at the steering wheel. "Dammit!" It was the old DeSoto.

Slowly he pulled the Chevy off the highway and parked about ten car lengths behind the DeSoto.

There was no sign of Duke, but he grabbed the breaker bar, just in case. There were no license plates. As he walked toward the car he followed a trail of fluid, which had turned the dirt a dark color. Big problem, probably fatal.

Marty found nothing inside the car. He took a deep breath and leaned against the front fender. Finding the DeSoto had been a shock.

His thoughts shifted to seeing Cathy and Duke together in the restaurant. Money had changed hands. They'd never intended to destroy the Roadster at the garage. When he hadn't noticed, they had checked on his progress at the garage to learn when he was leaving, and guessed the route he'd be taking.

It all added up. Cathy was probably up ahead somewhere, waiting. Duke was out there somewhere, too, but where? So much for a pleasant drive home.

"Aw, those sick screwballs," he muttered, on the way back to his car.

About to get into the Chevy, he got down on his knees, for a look underneath. When he'd slowed to stop, there had been a slight chirping sound. There it was, just as he'd suspected. A greasy universal joint. The tremendous force placed on the joint by that long climb was just too much. Cajon Pass got him, too. Damn!

Barstow wasn't that far ahead and he decided to chance it and keep going. Not long after, the chirping was louder and he could feel a slight vibration. More bad news.

Now his mind was focused on how best to remove the failing driveshaft without unhooking the trailer. The driveshaft looked like a pipe, about the diameter of a paint spray can, and maybe five feet long. It connected the engine and transmission to the rear axle and drive wheels. At each end of that five feet of pipe was a universal joint. It was the front joint that was failing and must be replaced to avoid a complete breakdown.

A few miles from Barstow the chirping was replaced by squealing sounds. Whenever possible, he shifted to neutral to take the load off the spinning driveshaft. "Come on, baby, hang on a little longer," he whispered.

"Welcome to Barstow," the sign read, and his tension eased. He pulled to a stop in front of an auto parts store and was able to get both front and rear universal joints. Following the part store guy's directions, he reached an auto repair garage.

So far, he'd been on the main drag in Barstow and he decided to take a calculated risk. He would make the repair on a back street, away from searching eyes.

His main concern was Cathy. She was out there somewhere, maybe trailing him. Reason enough to stay away from the auto repair shop. The Nomad had to be disconnected from the trailer, so it could be elevated on the lift. Sitting outside in the open would leave the Roadster and trailer vulnerable.

Instead, he found a backstreet not far from the repair shop and carefully drove the Nomad and trailer's curbside wheels up onto the sidewalk. Now the car was elevated just enough for him to slip under and remove the driveshaft.

With the car locked up, he carried the driveshaft and the new universal joints off in the direction of the repair shop. Explaining his dilemma to the mechanic got his job done in less than fifteen minutes. How lucky not to have started for home yesterday.

His plan had been to get off the road tonight by about six o'clock to make up for the lost sleep of recent days. Forget that, he told himself. Damn! Damn!

He found a gas station and while an attendant pumped gas, he circled the car watching for any signs of Cathy. After checking the engine fluids, he moved out into traffic.

As he came upon one last traffic light, he was gliding past cars in the lane to his right, while slowing for the red light. Then he saw it, a white Ford Falcon! Cathy! Before he could draw alongside, the female driver reached the intersection and the Falcon turned right, its tires squealing.

Was it Cathy? It sure looked like her. Had she seen him? Is that why she turned? Aw, knock it off, he told himself. What the hell's wrong with me? There must be thousands of white Ford Falcons out there.

So far, Highways 66 and 91 ran together as far as Barstow. To that point there were two lanes in each direction, but that was about to change. Highway 91 continued on to Las Vegas, while Route 66 split off to the east as a two-lane road. Soon, he was out in the boondocks.

He remembered there were few motels open at this time of year. A part of him wanted to find a motel right away and get some rest. A glance in the rear view mirror at his fragile treasure persuaded him otherwise.

More than anything, Duke wanted to get into Cathy's good graces. Chasing down Marty was the quickest way. She'd made it clear that pulverizing that old car would bring him rewards. In addition, there was the hint of a bonus if Marty suffered physical harm.

Duke was motivated.

Not knowing how much of a head start he had on Marty, he walked along the highway, altering his plans. Despite this setback, he was determined to fulfill his mission. Before long, he'd hitched a ride on an east-bound truck. Hours later, after crossing into Arizona, he saw a gas station up ahead. Pointing, he said, "How about dropping me off there."

He took up a position alongside the soda machine outside the gas station's office, and watched several dozen cars enter and leave. Eventually, a new black Cadillac pulled in and parked off to the side. Duke watched as the man struggled to get out. Once he was standing, Duke saw the man's enormous waist and smiled. Best of all, the fat man was alone.

Walking toward the Caddy, Duke began limping. "Excuse me, sir," Duke said.

The large man stopped wiping his sweating face. "Yeah, what?"

Duke smiled his best smile and asked, "I was wondering if you would give me a lift?"

"Where you goin'?" the man puffed.

"I live about ten miles up the road," Duke answered, pointing east.

The man studied Duke's face. "Yeah, stick around. I gotta find the crapper."

Watching the guy waddle off, Duke smiled again. Many minutes later the man, whom Duke guessed was in his fifties or sixties, appeared in the doorway of the station, eating a candy bar. He could barely fit through the door. Duke was excited by his good fortune.

As the man wedged himself into the car, Duke said, "I really appreciate this ride, mister. I usually just walk home, but my leg's giving me trouble today."

"What's wrong with it?" the man puffed, as he pulled out to the highway.

"It's messed up. Born with it," Duke explained.

"That's a tough break, kid," the man said.

Once they were up to cruising speed, Duke held out his hand and lied, "My name is Mike. Mike Wilson."

The man shook Duke's hand. "My friends call me Augie."

They made small talk, until Duke stopped rubbing his leg long enough to point to a dirt road up ahead.

"How far you got to walk?" Augie asked, slowing to stop.

"Oh, just a few miles, Augie."

"Sit tight, kid. I'll drive you up there."

"Hey, thanks a lot!"

Augie was either a careless or poor driver. Duke couldn't decide which. He just plowed ahead without slowing for a few dips along the way.

"When the hell they gonna pave this for you people?"

"It gets worse up ahead. Maybe you could just drop me here, Augie."

Augie's goodwill was just about exhausted and he slowed to a stop.

"Thanks, this is a big help."

Getting out, Duke waited a few seconds and then leaned down and looked at his benefactor. "Uh oh. You picked up a flat, Augie. It's this back one. I'm sorry."

"Aw, for ..." Augie bellowed.

His door swung open and he struggled out, cursing the whole time it took to make his way around the car. Duke met him at the rear of the car and stepped aside so Augie could have a look for himself.

"Son of a ..." Augie said. "There's nothing wrong ... Augh!"

Duke had rammed his foot into Augie's leg and the obese man's knee buckled as he crumbled to the sandy ground. "Are you crazy? Is this a robbery?"

"Good guess, Augie. Your wallet," he demanded.

"Sure, take it," Augie said with a scowl on his face as he held it up to his assailant.

Duke removed a wad of folding money and Augie's driver's license, then tossed the wallet back to his victim. He shrugged his shoulders and, sounding almost apologetic, he said, "I'm gonna need your car, too, Augie."

"Take it," he said, deciding it might save his life to get rid of this guy.

"Oh, not so fast. Get up. You're coming with me."

"Where? I can't stand up. I think you knocked my knee out of joint."

"I need to drop you a little farther from the highway. Can't have you runnin' to the cops until I'm long gone. Come on, get up."

Augie flopped onto the seat and Duke shoved his legs inside.

Duke soon found an even smaller dirt road and turned onto it. His captive had been silent for some time. Duke glanced over at him.

Augie was pressed back against the seat. The large man's face was now sweaty and a sickly grayish color.

Duke frowned. "What? You gonna kick off on me now, Augie?" He stopped the car and went around and opened the passenger door. After searching Augie's pockets, he said, "Here!" He removed two pills and stuck them into Augie's mouth, then stepped back and watched. Nothing.

Augie's breathing was still shallow. Duke was beginning to panic. He looked around. Nobody in sight.

"I can't stick around here," Duke said out loud. He reached in and grabbed Augie's arm.

There was a trench three feet deep that paralleled the dirt road. It went on for as far as he could see. He took Augie's arm and dragged him over to the ditch. Duke propped the unconscious man into a fairly upright position before climbing back onto the road. He sat there, staring at Augie. Seeing no improvement, he stood up and went back to the car. He thought about taking Augie for medical help.

How? he wondered. There was no way in hell he could get Augie out of that ditch. His other thought led to another dead end. Call for help. Where the hell is this? he asked himself. How can I call for help when I can't describe how to get to this place?

He went back to the trench. Maybe those pills helped. Augie's stomach was beginning to move again. He watched for a short time, then shrugged and drove off.

His financial status had taken a sharp turn for the better. He got just over three-hundred dollars from Augie and a car he was liking more and more by the minute. Looking around, his eyes fell on the glove box. He reached inside and his hand came out holding a gun, a revolver. Like a kid, he twirled it around his finger until it fell into his lap. He shoved the gun under the front seat. All he needed to do was mess up Marty's old car and go home to a grateful Cathy.

It wasn't chance, that he was driving a new Cadillac. For once, he planned ahead. It didn't set right, stealing a car from someone who might be as financially strapped as himself. But, there was a wildcard in this hijacking, he never figured. Augie's poor health.

He never figured. That pretty much summed up Duke's third-rate life. He never figured his rebellious behavior and disdain for authority would get him thrown out of school with a ninth grade education at the age of sixteen. He also never figured his expulsion from school was going to get him thrown out of the house only hours later.

"You're nothin' but trouble." his father yelled. Although it lacked eloquence, his old man, a drunkard, had pretty much hit the nail on the head. His mother not only approved, she pushed her husband to action.

Over the next eight years Duke had drifted to California and from one dead-end job to another. Lately, even those jobs became scarce owing to his run-in with the law and bouts of heavy drinking.

Reaching the highway, he sat there for a minute.

"Oh, Marty, where are you?"

# 13

It was nearly dark when a pick-up truck came along and its headlights illuminated Augie, struggling to get out of the trench.

"We've got to get you to the hospital, fella," the two rescuers said after seeing his condition.

Once there, Augie struggled to reach into his front pants pocket and pulled out a large roll of bills. He gave each of the men fifty dollars, but otherwise showed no gratitude for their assistance.

The hospital in Clemence was small. The doctor, dressed in white, came out pushing a gurney and all three pitched in to hoist Augie onto it.

After giving him a thorough examination, the doctor X-rayed his knee. It was badly sprained, but probably nothing more. It would be checked again tomorrow when the swelling would be less of a factor. With his knee treated, Augie was moved to a one-bed hospital room. Alone, he wasted no time in calling Los Angeles.

A male voice said, "Yeah, hello."

"It's me," Augie said.

"Augie, what's wrong?"

"I'm in a hospital. My new Caddy's gone, George."

"What? What the hell you mean, it's gone?"

"I felt like hell, my condition. I told you I should wait a while."

"Yeah, yeah. Is everything gone?"

"I'm sorry, George."

"Are you nuts? A hitchhiker?" George shouted after Augie filled him in.

Augie pulled the phone away from his ear. When the yelling ended, he shot back, "What? You want me to pass out along the road?"

"Augie, Augie! What... How ..."

"The damned twerp nearly busted my knee."

"I don't believe this!" George wailed.

After writing down the directions, he said, "All right. We'll leave now and see you in the morning."

Six o'clock came and went. Already in Arizona, Marty began to look for a place to get something to eat. He found a diner and hurried inside. Minutes later, he came out with a bag and coffee.

Underway again, his thoughts shifted to that icy mountain. The one that had nearly ended his life. It was just up ahead. He was squeamish about crossing it again at night.

He lowered his speed as he came to Clemence. There were two motels along this stretch, but only one was open for business. As he passed by, he shook his head. No good, he thought. Parking in there was too visible from the highway. What if I pulled around behind the one that's closed? he wondered. They wouldn't think to look there. Just then lights came on in one of the darkened units, so he kept on driving.

Thirty miles past Clemence, he rubbed his face with both hands. It was then that a car came up from behind and flew past him at high speed. He paid little attention. He remembered staying at a motel a few miles on this side of that mountain. It was set back from the highway and the place wasn't ablaze with outside lighting. He nodded. That's where he would stop for the night.

He was now traveling a long, flat and desolate stretch of road. Again he stretched and rubbed his face. Sleep was a problem, but that had been the case for the last four or five days. Tonight was supposed to change all that, but Duke's abandoned car put the notion of a full night of sleep to rest. He focused on shifting his thoughts to a different subject.

His was the only car on the road for as far as he could see in both directions. Minutes later he saw headlights coming his way. Marty played with the radio dial and after finding a good station he got comfortable.

"What the ..." Something didn't look right. He began to flash his high beams. "Get over!" he shouted several times.

He used both the car and trailer brakes to slow down. "Oh, boy!" The oncoming car was definitely in his lane! He continued to flash his lights and he pounded on the horn. The car was bearing down on him, moving fast.

The Nomad and trailer were now partway off the road. Still slowing. Still under control. The trailer was starting to slide sideways as Marty braced for a violent collision. Eeeeeyoww! The car flashed past and the Chevy was rocked violently by air turbulence.

Duke was petrified. All he'd intended was to scare Marty into wrecking his cars by crowding him off of the highway. Instead, he had nearly given himself a heart attack by grossly misjudging his speed and approach.

He struggled to get control of the car, jerking the wheel to the right, whereupon the car veered onto the road sideways and began a long skid. Terrified, his hands were all over the dashboard, grabbing at anything to brace himself.

Marty was out of his car now, watching in horror. "Turn the wheel! Turn the wheel!" he yelled, as if he could be heard over all the noise and distance.

Way down the road, he saw the car suddenly straighten out and drop completely off the pavement on the opposite side of the highway. The car was pitching up and down violently. Bam! Bam! Bam! He could hear the car repeatedly slam down on the barren, sandy, washboard surface.

Duke was no longer driving the car. He was simply along for the ride.

"Augh!" he wailed, sounding like a man falling from a skyscraper. The wailing stopped, when he was thrown sideways into the arm rest and then against the roof. He hardly felt the blows. His legs bounced around like those of a puppet until the Cadillac finally came to rest on the highway, mostly in the correct lane.

"Oh, shit!" Duke groaned, trying to sit upright. He was hurting everywhere. His hands moved to various parts of his body, eventually coming to rest gently on his right knee. That hurt was in a class by itself.

Getting back into his Chevy, Marty noticed a car coming toward him from the east. But it barreled past in spite of his efforts to slow it down.

Marty started turning the Chevy around.

Seeing this, Duke eased his damaged right leg to the gas pedal and drove off.

Unbelievable, Marty thought, shutting off the engine and getting out. Reaching in for his flashlight, he checked the Roadster for damage. Everything was okay, but he noticed the outside mirror on the Chevy was gone. Had the runaway car clipped it off? he wondered.

Leaning against the Chevy, Marty looked up the highway. What the hell happened? he asked himself. Maybe the poor guy suffered some kind of seizure. Maybe he fell asleep. Or, maybe he was drunk.

Back on the highway, the Chevy began to vibrate. Alongside the road again, he crawled under its front end. The flashlight revealed the small lead weight clipped to the left front wheel, to prevent vibrations like this, was missing.

Repair-wise, it was a nothing job, provided balancing equipment was available. For that he needed to find a garage or service station and have the wheel removed and rebalanced. It could wait until tomorrow. For now, he had to limp along the highway at something below vibration speed. Where the hell's that motel? he wondered.

Smoke was pouring out from beneath the Cadillac. "Aw, shit!" Duke bellowed. "Now what?" The car needed immediate attention.

Back a few miles was the gas station where he'd had the Caddy refueled. Where not that long ago he'd stood beside his car and watched Marty drive past.

The Caddy's engine sounded like a can of marbles being vigorously shaken as he rolled up to the open bay at the gas station. He turned off the ignition, but the engine kept making rattling noises and it shook the car for another five or six seconds.

It was taking a while for the dust and smoke to drift past the car. In seconds, the attendant came running outside with a fire extinguisher. Satisfied that nothing was on fire, he put down the extinguisher and approached the car. The young attendant leaned over to look inside.

"You okay, Mister?"

"Why?" Duke asked.

"Geez, what happened to your beautiful car?" the skinny young man asked.

"I got run off the road."

The attendant walked slowly around the huge car, looking at the damage.

"Mister, I'd say you're a helluva lot better off than this car."

"Yeah, yeah," Duke snapped. "See what you can do to get me out of here."

"Gladly," the kid shot back.

A crooked smile came over Duke's face. He liked that the kid didn't take any of his crap.

Standing up, the attendant said, "Damn, it's a real shithouse under there, mister. Let's have a look under the hood."

Working together, they finally popped the hood open.

"Holy shit!" the kid said in amazement.

The area between the grille and radiator was packed with tumbleweeds and other dead desert shrubbery. Sand was packed into every fin of the radiator, preventing air from circulating under the hood. For the next ten minutes, Duke and the attendant pulled debris from the engine compartment.

"I'm gonna have to jack up the car. That's probably my best bet," the kid said, before going into the station's service bay and coming out pulling a large floor jack.

Meanwhile, Duke went over to lean against the building trying to figure out what he would tell Cathy. She wouldn't want to hear how he bungled his great opportunity to finish things once and for all. He worked on a story, a snow job of epic proportions. How would she know any different?

The attendant finished up under the car in what Duke considered reasonable time. In all, there were three very impressive piles of desert flora extracted from the Caddy. Amongst them were flattened beer and soda cans and an assortment of paper and cardboard.

The attendant then dragged an air hose over and blew the sand from the radiator fins and the engine compartment.

"Damn, the radiator wasn't even busted," the kid reported. Seeing that Duke wasn't impressed, he said, "Why don't you see if it'll start?"

The engine fired up almost instantly.

"How much?" Duke asked, showing no appreciation.

"Well, let's see," the attendant said, looking at his watch. "That'll be eight dollars. Oh, and I've got to charge you two dollars for hauling all that stuff out of here."

"Two bucks?" Duke asked sarcastically. "What the hell's that for, funeral services?"

"It'll be my funeral, if the boss finds all this stuff here in the morning," the kid shot back.

"Aw, never mind," Duke said, pulling out a ten dollar bill, slapping it down on the Caddy's roof. The young man reached out, snatched the bill, and shoved it into his shirt pocket.

Moments later, Duke pulled out onto the highway and floored the gas pedal. "Two bucks my ass!' he carped.

The attendant watched the Caddy disappear into the night. Returning to the station office, he removed the ten dollars from his pocket and placed it carefully into his empty wallet.

# 14

Even at a reduced speed, Marty reached the motel in little more than ten minutes. There were about fifteen small cabins spread around the gentle hillside. He could park the car and trailer right alongside his cabin for security.

While checking in, he asked the desk clerk to assign him the cabin farthest from the road. Pulling his bag from the car, he looked around. Only a few cabins seemed occupied.

He exhaled loudly. Well, he thought, I've got to sleep sometime.

His sleep was troubled. During the night he awoke several times, imagining sounds. Around two in the morning, he sat upright in bed, straining to see in the semi-darkened room. The only light came from the bathroom through the partially opened door. Just for a moment, he thought he saw Duke sitting by the small table. It was Duke!

Startled, Marty started to bolt out of the bed.

"Set one foot on the floor and I'll clock you with this thing," Duke warned, holding what appeared to be Marty's breaker bar in a position to strike.

Marty settled back, his heart beating rapidly.

"So what now?" Marty asked as calmly as he could.

"You're gonna get out of bed, real slow, and get dressed."

"And then?"

"You and me are goin' for a ride out in the wilds, just like two buddies."

"This is about that roughing up in the parking lot, right?"

"Yeah, I owe you, tough guy. You made me look like a damn fool in front of her."

"Hey, you're the one who threw the punches," Marty replied.

"Yeah, but I was drunk. Let's see how you come out now, when I'm sober." Then he smiled, tapping his open hand with the heavy bar.

Marty pulled his sweatshirt down over his head and stood there, waiting.

"Okay, let's move it," Duke ordered, taking a few steps back out of the way.

They went outside, Duke following at just the right distance. The small motel sign was lit, but there was no sign of life.

"Let's have the keys, tough guy."

Marty handed them over when they got to the Chevy. Duke motioned for him to step away. Then he opened the door and flopped onto the back seat. He began to tap on the driver's seat with the weapon.

Marty got in.

"Screw around and you'll be fightin' me seein' double." Then he tossed the keys onto the front seat. "Let's go."

"Where to?"

"Just keep going until you see a dirt road. I'll tell you when."

They drove for nearly a mile before reaching the dirt road Duke wanted. Damn, Marty thought, we should be close to that mountain.

"Turn off right there and keep drivin'." After going a few hundred yards, Duke said, "Okay, this looks like as good a spot as any. Slow down easy and stop."

Sitting there quietly for a few seconds, Duke said, "Keys! Now slide over to that side and get out."

It was a cold, clear night. Duke quietly slipped the keys under the driver's seat and got out and headed for Marty. But Marty quickly moved around to the other side of the Chevy.

"Oh, Marty," he said in a mocking tone. "Watch this."

Bang! The sound shattered Marty's eardrums and he watched, not believing his eyes, as fluid streamed down onto the trailer's floor.

"Oops! Pretty chintzy car," he said, smirking.

Marty turned into a beast. A beast without self control. A beast without reason. Enraged, he charged, but stumbled before the heavy bar struck his lower back.

Thud! The deep sound of the blow spread across the quiet, uninhabited land. One of God's creatures had just been grievously harmed. There was no cry of pain. On this cold night, Duke, the human, had prevailed.

Before Duke could inflict further damage, the breaker bar began to crumble in his hand. Metal shavings fell to the ground like a plastic bag leaking rice. Duke's eyes rolled back in their sockets as he collapsed.

"Marty," a familiar voice said. Standing beside him was Pete O'Hara, the highway patrol cop from California whom he'd met while changing the tire for those two women. The one who'd given him the lead that led to the Roadster.

Pete knelt down and placed his hand on the injury. For an instant, intense pain shot through Marty's body, then it was gone. He could move again.

Marty rolled over and sat up. Pete was dressed all in white, some sort of robe, and he was surrounded by a dim, eerie glow.

"Pete?" Marty said weakly. "Where did you come from?"

"Come on, Marty, it's time to go."

"Go where?"

"I've come to accompany you home," he said, taking Marty's arm and pulling him to his feet. They left their feet and slowly floated upward. Marty looked down, watching the Chevy, the Roadster and Duke fall away.

"What's happening?"

"Look," Pete said, pointing to the east.

In the darkness, Marty could make out the lights of a car going up a mountain road. Just at that moment, icy rain hit his face. He closed his eyes because of the sting and when he opened them he was in his Chevy, towing an empty trailer. The windshield wipers were bouncing roughly across the ice covered glass. And Pete was sitting calmly in the passenger seat as the Chevy started its long descent.

"This is far enough," Pete said, reaching over to place his hand on Marty's shoulder.

They passed through the Chevy's roof as if it wasn't there and Marty looked down. The Chevy and trailer were hurtling wildly down the mountain, careening from one side of the road to the other and then disappeared into the darkness.

Now, he had the same glow as Pete. He felt different somehow, in a way he couldn't comprehend.

"This past week was some kind of dream, wasn't it?"

"No, it was real, but a few things were altered. There were many of us who were sympathetic and wanted you to have the chance to find your Roadster. Car lovers, like you." Pete smiled. "Let's just say the pleas fell on the right ears. Your time down there was extended until you returned to this mountain. That's when your time expired. I was sent to show you the way home."

"What's to become of my Roadster?"

"It's back in the Owens' garage, just the way you found it. Everything that happened since your accident, really only happened to you." Pete explained.

Their conversation was interrupted by a loud bell that jarred Marty. He was staring at a ceiling! Bolting upright, he slapped at the alarm clock. The Roadster!

# 15

Shaking off the cobwebs and the dream, Marty scrambled out of bed and jerked the door open. Gasoline fumes filled his nostrils. He jammed into his jeans and shoes and grabbed his jacket.

An uncapped, five gallon gasoline can lay on its side on the ground. Mostly empty! Its contents had turned the dirt muddy and dark under the trailer. He picked up the can, located the cap and set them aside.

Running to the back of the trailer, he removed the ramps and dragged them out of the mud. They had been positioned so the Roadster could be unloaded.

Hustling to the Nomad, he searched his pockets for the keys. Inside! He ran back into his room and grabbed the car keys from the dresser. His heart raced. He drove away from the muddy area, and got out to search for damage to his rig. He found none.

Disaster! Disaster! Images of an uncontrollable bonfire forced their way into his thoughts. After returning the trailer ramps to their normal position, beneath the trailer floor, he paused. How the hell did Duke install the ramps without waking me? They're awkward and heavy. After emptying what was left in the gas can into the Nomad's tank, he locked the car and went for a quick shave and shower.

Before leaving, he stopped at the motel office to pay his bill and tell them about the gas spill. The man at the desk thanked him and said he'd take care of it.

"How far is it to the nearest gas station?" Marty asked.

The man pointed west and replied, "Oh, about seven or eight minutes driving time."

At the highway, he turned west and backtracked to the gas station.

"Is this your can?" he asked the attendant.

"Yeah, looks like it," the attendant replied.

"Did you fill this can recently? It's important."

"See that guy getting into the car? He was on duty until eight this morning. Ask him."

Marty hurried over and asked, "Can you tell me if anyone filled this gas can last night?"

"Yeah, I remember," Joe said. "It was about one o'clock this morning."

"Do you happen to remember the car he was driving?"

"It wasn't a guy, mister. It was a woman. Pretty good lookin' one, too, if ya ask me. She was drivin' a Ford Falcon. A white one."

A chill came over Marty as Joe talked.

"I told her she'd be better off with a one gallon can, that a gallon of gas would be enough to get a car back here. No, she wanted the biggest can we had. So, that's what she got."

Before Marty could reply, Joe continued.

"Damn, fella, I hope there's not going to be any trouble."

"You didn't do anything wrong," Marty said. "I want to thank you for the information. Here, let me buy your breakfast." He held out two dollars.

Sheepishly, Joe accepted the reward.

"You know, I didn't think of this before, but there was one odd thing. It was a little after she left, when she came right back. She went right in there, to the ladies' room. Didn't come out for a long time. Things are pretty slow along about that time, so I took notice."

Marty was all ears.

"We clean the bathrooms before going off duty. The smell of gas was real strong in there, in the ladies' room. Must be she spilled gas on herself. When she came out, later on, her hair was plastered down, like it was wet. Plus, she was carryin' her coat in her hand. Damn! It was cold that time of mornin'. Is she anything to you?"

"Just trouble."

"Hope I'm not talking out of turn but, man, she's got some mouth on her, for a woman. When she left she went east."

Marty patted him on the shoulder. "Thanks, again."

He went into the station and asked the man on duty about balancing a wheel. The two worked together and Marty was soon on his way.

Back on Route 66, again, he settled in for another long day of driving.

Soaked with gasoline was not the time to light a match, he got that. But the thought of her setting up those ramps still bugged him. How could she do it without waking me? And, why set them up at all, to burn the Roadster? he wondered.

After a time, he began to reflect on his situation. By dumb luck, the Roadster ducked the ultimate disasters last night, a head-on crash, then a gasoline fire. He couldn't count on luck again, since he'd surely used it all up last night.

The nightmare last night had been a double feature. First there was the one starring Duke, then the second, Pete O'Hara. Another dream. What the hell's happening to me? Am I going nuts? he asked himself. Well, one thing's for damned sure. No more stopping at motels.

Before long, he approached his dreaded mountain and began the climb. When he reached the place where he'd collided with the guard rail post, he stopped. The damage he'd caused was minimal. The guard rail post was only slightly smudged with blue paint. At the top, he pulled over and got out for a few minutes, during which, he tried to shake the memory of this place out of his mind.

Down on the flatlands, he stepped up his speed. With some luck, he should reach Texas by nightfall, maybe even Oklahoma.

# 16

Duke sat on the edge of his bed and groaned when he saw how early it was. His eyes scanned the room, but he recognized nothing. Where the hell is this? he wondered.

Agony! Sheer agony! He was beginning to remember. After the Caddy was repaired last night, he'd stopped off at a saloon to calm his shaky nerves. He tossed a twenty down on the bar and didn't budge from his stool until everything was hunky-dory. After that came the poker game, same bar. The locals ended up with all the money he'd taken from Augie. Three hundred smackers. Three hundred reasons why he felt justified in calling that one local a card cheat.

Without thinking, his hand touched the side of his face. That cheatin' bastard sucker-punched me, he told himself, recalling the one punch knockout he suffered in front of the blood thirsty crowd of boozers.

He stood in front of the sink and looked into the cracked and cloudy mirror, trying to identify the face looking back. "Wait'll Cathy gets a look at this kisser," he moaned.

After washing up, he went shakily back to sit on the bed and sort out what he should do. Chasing Marty any further was finished business. Instead, he'd drive the Caddy over near the bus station and dump it.

Money! Duke pulled out his wallet. Empty. Groaning, he stood up and searched his pockets. Twenty-six dollars. He sagged back onto the bed wondering if it was enough to buy a bus ticket home. Getting up, he went outside and waited for his red eyes to adjust to the bright sunlight. His sore knee was on fire.

Right off, he noticed the Caddy's front tire was practically flat. The tire's sidewall was scrubbed down to where the cords beneath were visible. Standing there, staring at the tire for a time, helped to bring some things into focus. Last night, on the way here—wherever "here" was—he recalled colliding with a curbstone repeatedly. Limping badly, he made his way to the trunk. Inside was a large suitcase and a satchel. He popped the satchel open. "Holy shit!" he said, jerking upright.

Pulling the satchel out of the trunk, he quickly limped back into his room and sat down heavily. Opening the satchel, he stared down at more money than he could comprehend. Reaching in, he pulled out a bundle of neatly wrapped one-hundred dollar bills. The bag was filled to the top with them!

As he got over the initial shock, he dumped most of the contents onto the bed and began counting. The wrappers of each pack were plainly stamped, United States Treasury, along with the value of each tidy bundle. He arranged ten stacks of one-hundred thousand dollars each and there was still more money in the bag! He counted another half-million.

His mind was racing. What the hell was Augie doing with all this cash in the trunk of his car? And what about the gun? Pondering those vital points, he decided not to give a damn. This was the chance of a lifetime. A chance to start all over, someplace new, and live like a king. Besides, what was the alternative? Ask for a reward for returning the money?

All the pains were shoved aside. He forced himself to concentrate. Okay, he thought, I was here all night, the Caddy was parked right out in the open, maybe on the main drag, and no cops. How come? Duke went through a couple of scenarios, before settling on one he liked.

To be on the safe side, he supposed that Augie hadn't died. He sure in hell wouldn't tell the cops what happened. That would explain why the cops hadn't found the Caddy by now. His crime must not have been reported. Yeah, that's it. If the cops grabbed me, there goes Augie's money, he concluded.

He sprawled out across the bed and relaxed. He was glad Augie wasn't dead. There was never any intention of doing him any real harm, aside from the painful knee injury. And, since this morning, he was better able to appreciate Augie's suffering. He's probably up and around already, Duke imagined. That brought a smile to his face, as he stared at the water stained ceiling.

Finally, it occurred to him that he was probably being hunted! Right now! And not by the cops! Damn!

"I've got to lose the Cadillac! It'll connect me to Augie and this bread!" he whispered to himself. He then removed a few of the bills from one of the bundles and shoved them into his pocket while going through his other pockets to insure there was nothing of Augie's that would betray him. All he had left was Augie's driver's license. He stuck that into his shirt pocket for quick disposal later.

His new and improved plan called for him to drive the Caddy, flat tire or not, to the nearest cluster of parked cars and steal one of them. Failing that, he'd buy a used car and head east. Once I get to a big city, try and find me, he thought. After that, good times!

He got dressed, hobbled to the car and drove off. Minutes later, he was driving east, along Route 66.

Now, more himself, a few flaws in his escape plan surfaced. How was he going to trade the Caddy without ownership papers? Buying a car was no longer a financial problem, he thought, reaching over to tenderly touch the money bag. Still, he couldn't ditch this car and walk to a used car lot, not if the walk was more than twenty paces.

Instead, he watched for a place to ditch the car, out of sight from the highway. Better to take his chances hitchhiking. As each mile passed, without offering a suitable location to conceal the Caddy, he moved closer and closer to panic.

Augie was scared. He pulled up the bed sheet to mop his sweaty face. "Nine o'clock. Where the hell are they?" he muttered.

If the money wasn't recovered, his associates were certain to suspect him. They'd fight for the opportunity to make him confess his involvement in their imagined betrayal.

It was Augie's job to arrange deals between buyers and sellers.

He had the contacts. He knew many individuals who had a good deal of money to spend for the right merchandise. The risks were moderate and the rewards were tremendous. Nearing retirement, Augie had never once been involved in anything unsuccessful, until now.

A '56 Buick pulled into the hospital's small parking lot. Four men from Los Angeles, got out and stretched stiff muscles, before going inside to see Augie and figure out their next move. George led the way. He was the oldest, just past his fortieth birthday, and recognized as being in charge, at least by Doug and Harry. The three had worked with Augie for a number of years and this was the first time the group had faced the possibility of failure. They'd pulled off a number of jobs and, not once had anyone been hurt, a fact in which they'd taken great pride. While they brandished weapons, for the purpose of intimidation, none of their guns were loaded.

The robbery of the Los Angeles Air Freight Terminal was the biggest heist they'd attempted. All had agreed the job called for an additional man. Their window of opportunity was small and George went out and found Steve, a younger man, without thoroughly checking his background. The choice had been a serious mistake.

Steve was in his late twenties and, they later discovered, had a history of violence. He'd done a stint in prison for assault with a deadly weapon. That was the least of his crimes, but the only one that brought a conviction. He'd agreed to their rules, accepting George as the leader of the group and agreeing to carry an empty gun. When they'd been confronted by that terminal guard, George had begun to talk their way out of the situation. Based on experience, he'd have been successful.

But Steve didn't give him the chance. When the men raced from the building, the guard had been pistol whipped and left in a bad way. He was still in the hospital a week after the robbery. George, Doug and Harry agreed that, if the guard died, so would Steve. There was no way they would have the nut job on their team and, the minute this fiasco was cleaned up, Steve was history.

The four men filed into Augie's hospital room and surrounded his bed. George spoke first.

"I told the guys what you told me, Augie. What can you tell us about the guy who has our money?"

"He's about Steve's age, height and weight," Augie said, concealing his shaking hands beneath the sheets. Long black hair, combed back on the sides."

"What was he wearing?"

"Uh ... a brown leather jacket that looked too small for him. Blue jeans. He walked with a pretty bad limp. Said he was born with it." Augie glanced around. "He's not stupid. He suckered me good."

"What about the car?" George asked.

"He took the Caddy, along with my wallet."

"Which means he also took our money," Steve snarled.

"What the hell were you thinking?" Harry demanded. "Why'd you give the guy a ride in the first place?"

"I stopped at a gas station for candy. I was afraid of passing out. My condition, you know." He looked at George. "I told you it would have been better to wait a little longer." he said, attempting to defend himself.

Steve walked over and closed the door to the room, then turned on Augie.

"Listen, you fat load of shit, if we don't get that dough back, you'll be seeing me again. You'll be checkin' out, slow and painful." He frowned. "How come he let you live, anyway? He must have known we'd be coming after him."

"He didn't know about the money," Augie protested. "He just wanted my wallet and the car. Probably had no idea what he'd stumbled on. There's no way—"

"You know," Doug interrupted, "ever since I heard about this, I've been trying to figure the odds. You picked up a kid who needed a ride. He robs you and takes your car and, unknowingly, our money. What are the odds of that happening? A thousand to one? A million to one?

"Then, I'm thinking different odds. How about this? One of us set this up. How hard would it be to find a partner and do a two-way split? And, I'm thinking, I'll take those odds. We all knew when Augie was leaving, the route he was taking, the car he was driving.

"You know, when we catch up to this bozo, he's gonna talk. I wouldn't want to be in his partner's shoes." Doug looked around the room, his gaze lingering a bit longer on Steve than the others. With a jerky nod towards Augie, he left the room.

# 17

Duke was still trying to find a place to ditch the Caddy, when he spotted a small roadside diner. The closer he got, the bigger his smile. In front of the diner was the most beautiful '56 Chevy and trailer he'd ever seen!

He quickly pulled off the road and drove around behind the diner. Painfully, he got out of the Caddy and reached beneath the seat for the gun. With it stuffed behind his belt and covered by shirt and jacket, he grabbed the satchel and slowly made his way along the building to wait for Marty.

He didn't have long to wait. As Marty walked to his car, Duke hobbled out to intercept him.

"Could I talk to you for a minute?" Duke called out.

"I'll be damned!" Marty said, looking around for Cathy. "I was sure that, sooner or later, you'd turn up. You planning to follow me back to Pennsylvania? Duke, is it?"

"Yeah ... No! Yeah, that's my name. No, that stuff's over with. I don't want any more trouble." Then he threw his arms out to the side and looked down.

Marty studied him for a moment. There was no getting around it. This guy looked much the worse for wear and he moved like an old man.

"What happened to you?"

"My car broke down and ..." Duke looked around nervously. "It's a long story."

"I'm listening," Marty said.

"Some guys are after me. I got in a fight at a bar last night. They threatened to beat me senseless, so I took their car, but it crapped out on me. Could you see your way clear to—"

"Sorry, but I've got all the trouble I can handle, Duke."

"Just until I put some distance between me and them. Just drop me off at the first big city, that's all."

"Thanks to you, I missed out on a helluva lot of sleep—"

"That shit's over. Honest to God, I wouldn't be any trouble to you, I swear."

"How far behind are these guys?"

"They're right on my ass."

"Oh, no! Out of the question. What the hell's wrong with you? Haven't you caused me enough trouble?"

"If these guys catch up to me ... Please, you gotta give me a chance. Don't leave me here."

Marty was always a sucker, when it came to helping people. That's why he became a cop.

"Aw, shit!" He walked to the front of the Nomad and looked out at the vast open spaces. After a few seconds, he turned and nodded for Duke to get into the car.

Duke looked like a dirty, messed up little boy, sitting across from him, Marty thought. He sat there with the leather bag on his lap and both arms folded loosely, covering it.

Having traveled in silence for the first few miles, Marty asked, "Have you seen Cathy, since you left L.A.?"

"No. She sent me to do her dirty work." Looking down at his scruffy appearance, he said, "I got sidetracked. She's in L.A."

"I don't think so," Marty said, telling Duke about the gas can incident.

"No shit!" he said. "You know, I was pissed at you for taking her away from me, there for a while, but she came back. Well, she's talking to me again, at least. Turns out, she hates your guts. What'd you do to her?"

Marty told about the night at the dance.

"Ain't she something?" Duke replied. "Hey, that's nothin'. You know about us? Cathy and me?"

"Only that you were after her."

"That's what she told you?" Duke squinted and looked out the side window. "I don't care if you believe this or not, but Cathy and me used to go together. That's right! And, you know ... We became close. We were very close, get it?" Duke smirked. "We lasted about four, maybe five months.

"That," he continued, "was when she walked in and caught me with another gal. Cathy went nuts. She would've killed Sherri-Lee, if I hadn't pulled her off and tossed her out."

"That was the end of you two?"

Duke shook his head. "Sometimes, I wished it was. One thing was for sure, I shot to the top of her Drop Dead List. It's a long one. Hell, half the population of the city must be on it.

"I called her a bunch of times, tryin' to square myself, but she'd hang up. Finally, after a couple of weeks, I went to the airport and waited out by her car. A few times, she smiled and I thought I was gettin' somewhere, but when she saw a couple of guys walking our way, she went nuts. Started screamin', dropped to the ground and ripped at her clothes.

"All I tried to do was get her to stop. Those two guys were all over me. I must have said, 'I didn't do nothin', a hundred times that night." He shrugged his shoulders. "Three and a half years in the can."

"What about your lawyer?"

Duke sneered. "He was just out of school, for Christ sakes. He didn't know shit. I told him we'd been doing it plenty of times before that night. She said I was lyin'. My lawyer couldn't find anybody who ever saw us together before her parking lot Academy Award number. We never went out much. Her choice. I figured she didn't want to be seen with me. Anyway, when I did have money, some bartender ended up with it. Even I understood I was up shit's creek before the trial got started."

"Going to prison didn't tick you off, even a little?"

"Hell, yes! At first, it did. After I got out, I went around to see her. Yeah, I threatened to mess her up for lying about me. That's when she moved in with those old geezers over at your garage.

"I got no family and only a few bartenders for friends, when I have money. Just her. I was always crazy about her. You know, there were times, um, not many, when she was really, eh, nicer than a chump like me deserved. She could be a real soft and gentle woman, when she put her mind to it."

He looked over at Marty, "No, not that stuff. I never knew it could be like that. No one ever made me feel that way. Those quiet times together, just holdin' her, that's what I remembered when I was away. I came back for more of 'em. I figured I'd earned it."

Then he shook his head. "She's got a screw loose. Probably a bunch of 'em."

Marty looked over at his passenger. The poor slob. Before the dance, he never would have believed anything this guy said. But now, nothing he'd just heard raised an eyebrow. How screwed up she must be, to send an innocent guy to prison.

Duke broke the silence. "Me? I'm going to Boston, or maybe New York." He sat there grinning.

"Wait a minute. Remember, I'm dropping you off at the first big city. That was the deal."

Duke looked over at him and grinned. "I know." Then his hand came out of the bag clutching a pack of hundred dollar bills.

"Where did you get that?"

Duke tipped the opened bag and showed him the rest of the money.

"Damn! So that's the reason you're being chased?" Not waiting for an answer, Marty was shaking his head. "You lied, back there at the diner, didn't you?" Again the answer was obvious and he wondered why he bothered to ask. Now, he suddenly felt chilled.

"I had to, or you wouldn't have helped me."

The answer was met with a glare.

"Okay, the truth. I took this from a guy called Augie. I swiped his car yesterday and this morning I found this in the trunk," Duke said, looking down at the bag.

"So, where's Augie now?"

"Hell if I know. Either where I left him, or at a hospital."

"You hurt him?"

"I messed up his knee a little. I couldn't let him run out to the highway and flag down help, now could I?"

"Well, if Augie's in the hospital, who's after you?"

Duke shrugged.

Suddenly, the lingering chill worsened. Marty whacked the steering wheel. Duke was startled.

"By any chance, would there be one and a half million in that bag?"

Duke covered the bag with both arms. "How could you know that?"

"Oh, Jesus!"

"What? What?" Duke said.

"You know where that money came from?"

"How could I?"

"Soon after I came out here, the story was on the radio every fifteen minutes. Four guys knocked off the Freight Terminal at the L.A. Airport, for exactly the amount you have there. They knocked hell out of a guard before it was over."

"Okay then, so there's four guys after me."

"No. There's four guys after us."

"What're you talkin' about?" Duke said, annoyance in his voice.

"We've got to go back."

"The hell you say! Go back where?"

Marty slowed the car and turned onto a dirt road.

"Keep going!"

Too late. Marty pulled out of sight before stopping.

"Look Duke, if the guys who are after you pass that diner we just left, unless they're blind, they'll see Augie's car. They'll search for you and then cross the highway to ask those two hitchhikers questions. They'll be told you got into this car and headed east. We've got to back and get those hitchhikers away from the diner."

"What if we're too late? What if those hitchhikers already got a ride? What if we pass Augie and his boys on the way back?"

"Oh, great!" Marty mumbled when he saw the gun pointed his way.

"I'm gettin' the hell out of here. Do you understand?"

"Dammit, Duke. The money's not worth getting killed over."

"Says you."

"Are all of those bills brand new?"

"What about it?"

"If you'll check, their serial numbers are consecutive. They're registered. Spend any, and the Feds will be down on you in no time."

"Okay, so I lay low for a few weeks—"

"More like five years, maybe ten. Augie was taking that money somewhere to sell, for maybe fifty cents on the dollar. Those guys knew better than to spend any of it."

Duke slumped in his seat, slowly shaking his head. He'd heard about the robbery, but somehow it never entered his euphoric mind. He now realized he should have known better. Good things, like this windfall, didn't happen to guys like him. All he had left was his stinking life. It wasn't enough.

"Get out of the car," Duke ordered. "Over there," he motioned. Duke slid over behind the wheel and started the car. When the dust settled, he was out of sight.

Walking quickly, Marty followed along the dirt road for nearly fifteen minutes. Then he spotted his Nomad, coming over the rise, but without the trailer and Roadster! Heavy clouds of dust filled the air as the Chevy sped past.

Now running, Marty reached the top of the hill. Off in the distance, some three or four hundred yards, was the trailer and Roadster. Gasping for air, he circled the trailer then sat on the trailer fender.

"Dammit! Dammit! Dammit!" he shouted. He smacked his forehead with the palm of his hand. "How could I have been so stupid?"

After a minute he took stock of his situation. On the front of the trailer he noticed his coat, suitcase and toolbox. He gratefully put on the jacket and his hand slipped into a pocket, where he'd kept the Roadster's keys. At least he could start the car without hotwiring it.

Grumbling, he'd started to undo the clotheslines holding down the Roadster's covering. The covering at the back of the car had already worked loose. With the car's wrappings on the ground, he did another inspection. He exhaled loudly when he found no damage. The Roadster was now his transportation.

He put the toolbox inside the car. It barely fit. It really belonged in the rumble seat compartment, but the thought of the heavy metal box scraping across the unblemished paint settled the matter. Besides, his suitcase took up most of the room back there.

About to leave, his eyes fell on the trailer's license plate. He took the time to remove it, in case there was no reason to come back.

Slowly, so as not to stir up dust, he drove back to the highway and decided to go back to the diner. His immediate concern was to thwart the criminals in any way possible.

Maybe it was the cop in him, but he saw the robbers as more criminal, dangerous and illusive than Duke. They got under his skin. They shouldn't be allowed to recover the stolen money. Taking away the link to Duke, who was the lesser of two evils, was the right thing to do.

For the next ten minutes, Marty forgot all his troubles. Over the past sixteen years, he'd dreamed of sitting behind the wheel of his illusive Roadster and actually driving it. Now, it was happening! The Roadster was a delight. It rode beautifully and he soaked up the sound of the small V8 engine. He reveled at the sight beyond the windshield, the small, streamlined headlight set snugly in the valley between the gleaming black hood and the gracefully creased fender. How it all came back. He was a boy, again! It was magic! What a spectacular drive!

Too soon, the magic faded when the diner came into view. There was a lone hitchhiker standing beside the road.

"Need a lift?" he asked the man.

"Yeah, that would be great!"

The man got in and carefully slipped his feet around the toolbox before closing the door very gently. Marty smiled. This guy had class.

The Roadster accelerated up to cruising speed, the man watching Marty's every move.

"Damn, what I'd give to have a car like this."

Marty smiled and nodded. After the introductions, came the standard car questions. He took his time and answered them to Jay's satisfaction. Then he took his turn.

"Not much luck hitchhiking today, huh?" Marty asked.

"The guy out here with me got a ride a few minutes ago, but there was only room for one," Jay said, "Earlier, there was a car that stopped, but all they wanted was information."

"Information?"

"Yeah. They spotted a Caddy behind that diner and wanted to know where the owner was. Good thing the owner took off when he did. Those guys made a real mess of his car, getting the doors and trunk open. Did you notice it?"

Marty slowly shook his head.

"I could have told them about the guy, but they were snotty pukes. I told them nothin'.

The guy out here with me spilled his guts though. They didn't give him a ride anyway."

"Sounds like the ones who cut me off earlier. Were there four of them, in a blue '59 Dodge?"

"No, it was a black '56 Buick, but it was filled with four pukes though."

Marty nodded. "By the way, how far you going?"

"Albuquerque. Then north to Denver. That's home. I was out in Hollywood for the past three years. Gave myself three years to break into the movie business. So, now, it's home and a real job."

The gasoline situation was now a major concern. The only gas he'd put into the Roadster was the dollar's worth he took to the garage in a can. Barely four gallons. He'd better find a place to fill up, and soon.

The two men said little more, before Jay dozed off.

A small town came into view. They must have a gas station. Minutes later, Marty eased up to the pumps. After waiting a few seconds he went to the station office, where he was met by an elderly man.

"Comin'. Be right there," the old timer said. "Fill her up, young fella?"

"Uh, yes, sir. Okay if I do it?"

"Yep. Still gotta charge ya full price though."

Marty had pumped five gallons before the old man reached the rear of the car and stood there looking down, as if mesmerized.

He muttered what sounded like, "Somethin' don't make no sense." The scrawny old gent looked to be at least eighty years old, Marty guessed.

"What year is this?" the old-timer asked.

"Nineteen thirty-six." The answer set off another round of mumbling.

"No, not the car! I mean, what year is it, now!"

"Nineteen sixty-one."

"I knew that! I knew it all along!" the old man chuckled, as he slapped his leg excitedly. "There for a time, I thought I caught amnesia, or something," he confided.

The old man looked around, then whispered hoarsely, "You're a mite behind on your license plate, Bub. Hereabouts, you gotta pay for new one's every year. How's it work in your state?"

"The same." Marty smiled when he finally caught on that this was about the Roadster's 1941 license plates.

"Don't the law ever stop ya, on account of 'em?"

"Not so far, but I plan on getting new ones first chance I get."

The sound of gas gurgling signaled the tank was nearly full.

"Keep your eyes peeled for the law, young fella. They're sneaky buggers."

After paying for the gas, Marty waved to the old character, as he pulled out onto Route 66.

"I'm just making conversation, Marty, nothing more, but I've been wondering why you went out of your way to give me a ride."

What the hell, Marty thought, he was never going to see this guy again. He launched into the story of his trip and his falling out with Duke and Cathy. Instead of mentioning the robbery money, he gave Duke's original version, that those four guys were chasing him, because he stole their car. After all, what did he really know about Jay? The last thing he needed was for this guy to start acting weird over a lot of money.

"Damn, last night must have been a real bitch. Did you call the cops?"

"No, what could they do, really?"

"What's to stop her from pulling the same thing tonight?"

"No more motels on this trip." Looking at his watch, he added, "And, I'll have to find a place to get off the road by nightfall. If she caught up to me in the dark, especially from behind, I'd be neck deep in quicksand. That reminds me. She could jump us at any time and turn this car into a pile of twisted metal. We can't outrun her. You might want to think about getting another ride at the next town, Jay."

Marty's thoughts turned to her catching him during daylight. Sure, the Roadster was a hot little firecracker in its day and, even now, its eighty-five horsepower engine moved the car along very nicely. It steered and stopped okay, too, under normal circumstances. Still, the Roadster would be over-matched. Its magnificent looks would count for nothing. Twenty-five years of advanced automotive technology was in the car she was driving.

Jay broke the silence. "Damn! You're in a real bind, all right. But, maybe I could help. If we do come across your Chevy before Albuquerque, I could drive it back to your trailer and you'd be in good shape again."

Marty had pretty much given up any hope of reclaiming the Nomad and trailer, but he was intrigued by the offer. Suppose he let Jay drive the Roadster west. If Cathy turned up, he could run interference with the Nomad. Then he remembered how she'd smashed into the garage. What if she somehow smashed into Jay? He'd be the one helpless. On the other hand, what if Jay drove the Nomad? But could he keep Cathy away from his treasure?

Marty looked over at his passenger and smiled. "I really appreciate the offer, Jay. Thanks. If we come across the Nomad in running condition, I just might take you up on your offer."

# 18

A large white truck pulled off the highway and stopped in the diner's parking area. Charlie and Morg had talked it over and decided it was time to call J.C. back in Los Angeles. Charlie lost the coin-toss.

"J.C., it's Charlie."

"Where are you guys?"

"Some little berg in New Mexico. I didn't catch its name."

"You got some good news for me, Charlie?"

"No, not yet. We had a chance at the Roadster last night, at the kid's motel, but it didn't work out."

"Why? What happened?"

"Damned if I know, J.C. We located his rig at this motel, way out in the sticks. He rented a cabin as far from the highway as he could get. He had that car wrapped up like some kind of Christmas present. And it was lashed down with chains, like it was the Queen Mary or somethin'."

J.C. felt the blood run to his head as he listened.

"That was far as we got, when this car pulled in from the highway and parked near our truck. Must be midnight, or so. Up walked this woman who looked over the station wagon and pulled up the Roadster's cover in a few places and then took off. So we moved. We had the ramps in place and, just when we were about to go under the trailer to remove the chains, Morg told me she was back again. We got out of there."

"What now?"

"So help me, J.C., she's lugging this big-ass can of gas. I almost felt sorry for her, the way she struggled. Then she tried to hoist the can up onto the trailer."

"Why? I don't understand."

"All I know is, she didn't intend to fill the gas tank. Next thing I know, there's gasoline all the hell over the place. Then she ran to her car and beat it.

"She was going to torch that Roadster, J.C. Morg agrees. Thing was, the dizzy broad must not have had matches. She left a swamp of gas. One spark. We got the hell out of there."

Charlie could hear J.C. groaning.

"Boss, that was the good news."

"What the hell was good about—"

"Maybe twenty minutes ago, the kid blew by us, doing at least eighty. He—"

"Charlie, you guys been drinking? There is no way in hell that car is going to pull that trailer at eighty miles an hour! Nothing close."

"That's the whole point, J.C. There was no trailer, no Roadster. Just the Nomad."

"That's crazy! You got the wrong car."

"I don't think so. Morg and me saw the Pennsylvania license plate and the off color blue front fender on that car, just like you said."

"Well, what the hell did he do with my car?"

Charlie exhaled loudly. "We think he must have sold it."

"No! Not a chance!" J.C. said. "I saw the look on his face. No amount of money was going to pry that car from him. No, he didn't sell it."

"Want us to keep going? We're not very optimistic."

"Um, I ... Finish out the day and if you don't come across him, give it up and come on back."

"You got it, J.C."

Thanks, and wishes of good luck flowed in both directions at Albuquerque when Marty dropped off Jay. Now, it was official. The Nomad and trailer were gone for good. He'd report the Nomad stolen, but the trailer had to be a write-off. Of the two, he was saddened most by the loss of the trailer, a gift from his dad.

Marty stopped an hour later at a roadside diner and then topped off the Roadster's gas tank. There was a third stop when he noticed several Indians along the roadside selling all sorts of things from their stand. He bought their heaviest blanket and a small embroidered pillow.

Duke had been pushing the Nomad very hard for several hours. This time, when he checked the rearview mirror, he saw a black car far behind. Minutes later, it appeared the car had gained on him.

The two cars continued across the vast open spaces for another twenty miles before Duke blew through a small settlement at twice the legal speed limit. A highway patrol officer witnessed this lawlessness and quickly took up pursuit.

The black Buick had closed the gap to one-half mile, before backing off, when the patrol car entered the highway up ahead.

That Marty had reported the Nomad stolen was the first thought that came to mind, when Duke saw the police car. He continued on as before for a few minutes, before making up his mind that he couldn't outrun the cop.

Overly anxious to stop, Duke jammed the four speed transmission into third gear and the Nomad reacted violently. Oil, anti-freeze and metal fragments spewed onto the roadway, sending the speeding car off into the sandy surroundings. The Nomad rolled over a few times before coming to rest on its four wheels.

The officer found Duke alive, but unconscious. The seatbelt had done its job. However, he was trapped inside by the steering wheel and dashboard, which had firmly pinned his legs against the seat. The L.A. four left the Buick and rushed to join the officer and another motorist at the wreck site.

"An ambulance is on the way," the officer told the civilians.

The four pursuers moved around the car eyeing its contents, but without satisfaction.

Others had arrived and tried to help free the victim.

****

Back on the road, with little daylight remaining, Marty slowed, when he came upon the many cars lined up on both sides of the highway. He found the black Buick among them.

"Aw, no! No!" he said out loud, as he located a parking space and hurried to the wreck.

"What happened?" he asked a bystander.

"It was awful. I was coming from the east and that car was coming toward me. It was really moving. That cop was chasing it, I think. Then I saw flames and smoke coming from underneath and it began to swerve all over the road. I thought I was a goner. But then it skidded sidewise and left the road. Poor fella. I never knew a car could bounce like that."

"Is he alive?"

"So far. But he's still stuck in there.

Marty scanned the crowd, looking for a group of four. There they were, standing off from the wreck. He joined those at the Nomad to see if he could help.

"Anyone have a long bar, or length of pipe we can use as a lever?" he asked.

"I do," a man called out. "Be right back."

The ambulance arrived and the attendants worked on Duke. Finally he was pulled from the Nomad and whisked off to the hospital.

As it turned out, Marty got a little too involved in Duke's extraction, which was noted by George, the leader of the L.A. four. More than that, he also noticed Marty and the officer discussing something afterwards.

By now, most of the curious had moved on and Marty headed for his car. George watched as Marty got into the Roadster, before returning his attention to the Nomad and the money.

The four men from L.A. were the last to leave. After ransacking the Nomad and coming up empty, they returned to the Buick. George turned the car around and headed for a motel. Tomorrow they'd visit the accident victim at the hospital and make themselves known to him.

"What the hell did that asshole do with our dough?" one of them asked.

Moments later, George braked hard, almost skidding off the road.

"I'll be damned!" he yelled, slamming his hand against the steering wheel.

"What? What's happening?" the one riding shotgun asked.

"That's it. It's gotta be."

"What the hell you talkin' about, George?"

"Remember what that hitchhiker said this morning?"

The others looked at each other, but remained silent.

"He said the guy was pulling a car trailer with the Nomad. What kind of car would be towed and covered over?"

Seeing all the blank stares, George added, "An old car! Was I the only one to notice the old car back there, and how the driver was all over the wreck, trying to do everything?"

"Yeah, I did. They were partners," a voice from the back seat said, excitedly.

"The guy in the Roadster has all our dough," another said.

George had already made a U-turn and they raced to the east. "He's only got a little head start on us, and in that old car, we'll be all over his ass in no time," he assured the others.

# 19

$S$anta Rosaria was only a ten minute drive and when Marty reached the town, he turned onto a residential street looking for a place to spend the night. He found an alley that paralleled the street and parked between two private garages.

As tired as he was, he couldn't sleep. Something was bothering him and in time, it became clear. Back at the accident site, he noticed one of those four Buick guys watching him. What if he puts two and two together? Damn, they might be looking for me right now, he thought.

On the way to Santa Rosaria, he remembered seeing a dirt road, not more than a mile from here. They'd never think to search there, he reasoned. Moments later, he had the Roadster running and left the area to return to the highway. Nearing the main road, he braked hard, when he saw the Buick slowly cross his path, going west. He moved closer to the intersection and watched, as the Buick slowed to a stop, before turning onto a residential street, on the other side of the highway.

Marty waited about thirty seconds and then turned west on the highway. Momentarily turning off his lights, he slipped past that street, before speeding off to find his dirt road.

Only moments after leaving Santa Rosaria, he passed an oncoming large white truck. A truck occupied by Charlie and Morg, two of J.C.'s boys. Charlie smiled as the Roadster sped past.

Turning to Morg, he asked, "So which are we, lucky or good?"

Morg was no longer smiling. "We're lucky. You know what I think? I believe that when you have real good luck, like this, you're in for some real bad luck. Luck has a way of balancing out over a guy's life.

"Charlie, let's forget we ever saw that car, and just go the hell home. If we don't get our hands on it, then it wouldn't count as good luck. See what I mean? Look, how's J.C. gonna know any different? What the hell, he's already got three of those cars anyway. What's he need another one for?"

"You gotta be kidding! Morg, we got it made with J.C. You want to jeopardize that? Let's keep him happy. Come on, forget all that luck crap."

Morg slowly nodded his head. " Maybe you're right, but I still don't like it."

Marty was growing anxious. "Come on, where the hell is it?" he said softly. More than once, his head snapped to the right or left at some imaginary danger.

"There it is," he whispered, as he turned off the highway.

He soon found what looked like a good place to spend the night. Light snow flurries had begun and the winds rocked his car. At first, he had a little trouble settling down. But he soon relaxed and the symphony of leaking wind noises, accompanied by the gentle rocking, carried him off to sleep.

A voice shouting "Hey in there!" startled Marty out of a fitful sleep and he jumped again, when he saw a face peering through the windshield.

"Damn," Marty said, expecting the worst.

"Hold up, mister!" the voice called out.

Marty cautiously opened the door and got out, wondering if this was another version of that dream from last night and the other times back in Chastaine.

"Who are you?" he asked.

"We live here," the man said, as he pointed up the road. "What are you doing out here?"

"I was hoping to spend the night here," he answered, noticing an older woman standing nearby.

"Son, you'll freeze to death out here! This is New Mexico."

Marty's neck felt cold and his face and hands were already numb. He began to shiver.

"Look, young fella, why don't you come on up to the house and get warm?"

In no shape to be indifferent, Marty replied, "I'd really appreciate that, sir."

In a few minutes, inside their home, his face and hands began to sting.

"Let's get you warmed up, young man," the wife said, as she adjusted the water temperature at the kitchen sink.

It was nine o'clock. He'd been asleep for barely an hour. These people probably saved my life, he thought.

Chet introduced Ida and Marty introduced himself.

"Marty, are you hungry?" she asked.

She prepared ham and eggs for him, with hot coffee. During the meal, feeling more at ease, he told them about his trip out West, the Roadster find and his current difficulties.

"Good Lord," Chet said, "That's the damnedest thing I ever heard. Sounds like you got half the state of California after ya." He got up from the table and left the room, coming back minutes later with two rifles and a box of ammunition. "Let 'em come," he snorted.

"Why don't you put your little beauty out there inside the barn," Chet offered. "It'll stay dry and out of sight."

Marty smiled for the first time in days.

When the two men returned to the house, Marty set his suitcase next to the couch that Ida had made into a bed. It was all ready for him.

Ida said, "It's not much, but at least you won't freeze, Marty. Good night."

"Good night, ma'am. I thank you both for everything."

Marty checked his wallet for cash. One hundred and eighty-nine dollars.

He took out fifty dollars and placed the money under a potted plant on the window sill.

In the darkness and quiet, he thought about their kitchen.

Everything was clean and orderly, but it looked out of time. The appliances, furniture, even the sink, took him back to his childhood. Twenty, twenty-five years ago, that's where this kitchen is from, he imagined. He already liked the couple, but their situation troubled him.

# 20

"What's your next move, Marty?" Chet asked after breakfast.

Marty shrugged. "I plan to give that a whole lot of thought this morning, Chet."

"That's a peach of a car you've got. Ain't seen one like it in a long time. Any chance of gettin' a look at her in the daylight?"

Marty eased the Roadster out of the barn and gave them the grand tour. Ida and Chet both got to sit behind the wheel. He opened the hood and Chet checked out the engine compartment.

"Clean as a whistle under here," he said with a smile.

"Oh, wait till you see this!" Marty said, as he went around and lifted the Roadster's Rumble seat lid. "Want to try it out, Ida?"

Chet looked in. "Naw, better not," he told Ida.

Puzzled, Marty leaned over and looked inside. There on the floor was Duke's bag of money!

With the show over, he backed the Roadster into the barn. Removing a screwdriver from his toolbox, he popped the valise open. The money was still inside. He left the bag open, but closed the compartment's lid and followed his hosts into the house.

Leaning against the sink sipping coffee, Marty asked himself how could this have happened. It had to be yesterday, on that dirt road, when Duke commandeered his rig. That's when Duke put the money into the Roadster. But how could I have missed seeing it, he wondered. He recalled putting his suitcase into the compartment yesterday. I had to have seen it. And last night in the dark barn ... But why did Duke leave the money? I don't get it.


Marty finished his coffee and told his hosts needed to take a walk and do some heavy thinking.

Walking across an open field, he turned his thoughts to Ida and Chet. He wanted to somehow repay them for saving his life and for their kindness. The money discovery this morning might be part of the solution. But whatever he did, it had to happen quickly. If Duke survived the crash, he could make things a lot better for himself by disclosing the whereabouts of the money. And those four men from L.A. were out there looking for him. They were not likely to give up easily.

In close to an hour, he came up with a number of ideas, but they were rejected as unworkable, or downright illegal. All but one.

Returning to the house, he asked if he could use the phone to make a long distance call.

"Of course," Ida said, reaching into her apron pocket to remove the fifty dollars. Marty, this is too much."

"I haven't left yet, Ida." He smiled.

"Operator, I'd like to be connected with the Los Angeles Field Office of the United States Treasury Department."

Ida and Chet got up to leave the kitchen, but Marty motioned for them to stay. "No problem," he said, shrugging his shoulders.

"Yes," Marty said, "I'd like to talk with the agent in charge of the Los Angeles Airport Terminal robbery of last week. Okay, I'll wait."

In a few moments agent Jerry Wynn came on the phone and Marty identified himself.

"So you're a state trooper?"

"Yes, sir. That's right." Marty replied.

"So what have you got for us?" Jerry asked.

Marty told him the whole story, hoping he hadn't left out any details. When he had finished, there was dead silence.

"Are you there?" Marty asked.

"Yes, I'm here," Jerry replied. "I'm just stunned. We don't often get calls like this. Where are you?"

Marty gave him the details and Jerry put the phone down for a few minutes. Marty waited, smiling over at Ida and Chet.

"Okay," Jerry said, coming back on the phone. We're flying into Albuquerque and should reach you by one o'clock."

"I'll be here."

Twenty minutes before they were expected, a car pulled up in front of the house and two well-dressed men got out. On the porch, Marty introduced himself to Jerry and his associate, Elliott. Then Marty introduced the agents to Ida and Chet.

Marty guessed the feds were in their mid-thirties as the three men walked slowly out into a field behind the house.

"Ida and Chet are two really terrific people," Marty began.

"Yes, it seems so," both agents agreed.

Marty told how he nearly froze to death the night before and how they'd rescued him. He glanced around the ranch. "This place must have really been something twenty years ago. Ida told me they once had nearly three hundred head of cattle. Fever got them, she said. It must have been quite a blow."

"Yes, I can believe that." Jerry said.

In the daylight, the place looked pretty run down.

"Okay, here's the deal," Jerry said steering the conversation to the business at hand. "We don't ordinarily get involved in robberies. However, that Augie character has been on our wish list for a long time. We believe he's the middle man in the counterfeiting operations out our way. Now, if we can implicate him in this robbery, he might be persuaded to give us some names. The guy could open a floodgate of arrests."

"And, if you can get the robbers, they could confirm Augie's involvement."

"That's it. Right now, two of our guys are looking for Augie along that section of Route sixty-six you told me about earlier. Trouble is, we've got to turn up his robbery associates pretty quick or cut Augie loose, again."

"Maybe I can help."

The three men began walking again. Marty led the way to the barn to show off his treasure.

During the showing, Jerry said, "We're glad you called us Marty, but why didn't you just call the highway patrol?"

Marty played his only bargaining chip. "The highway patrol doesn't offer rewards."

The agents were surprised by his answer.

"Marty, you should know that police officers can't ..." Both agents began to smile and nod. "You're talking about a reward for Ida and Chet," Jerry said.

"Is it possible ?" You know, Chet was the one who discovered the valise?"

"It's possible, but . . . Valise?"

Marty opened the rear compartment lid and nodded. "I'd bet it's all there."

"But how...? Where did...?"

Marty then filled them in and asked, Suppose Augie's prints are on this bag, or those bills. Would you say his prints were pretty damning evidence?"

Jerry smiled. "Air-tight."

"I'll call it in and get someone to come pick it up," Elliott said.

The agents smiled and patted Marty on the shoulder. "You really know how to make a guy's day special," Jerry said.

"Will you try to do something for those folks, Jerry?"

"I give you my word. Anything else?"

As they headed for the house, Marty replied, "I want to get those four guys off my back.

"When are we going to start after them?" Marty asked.

"We?" Jerry asked.

"You bet." Marty said.


Marty opened the door and followed his new friends inside. After coffee, Jerry made several calls to Los Angeles. He requested someone be sent to pick up the recovered money and run some finger prints. Next, a call to touch base with his boss and to insure that word of the recovery of the robbery money wasn't disclosed for several days. He then called the closest highway patrol office for assistance.

Turning to Elliott, Jerry said, "Let's be on the safe side, call the Motor Vehicles Department in Harrisburg and ask them to remove Marty's auto registration information from their files immediately. Tell them we'll get the formal request out a.s.a.p."

"I'm impressed," Marty said.

"How long can you stick around to help us with this?"

"Well, I've got to report for my new assignment on Monday. Today's Thursday. Actually, I've got to get the Roadster home and my butt back to southwestern Pennsylvania by Sunday night. So, I've got to get out of here no later than noon, tomorrow."

"Aren't you cutting it pretty close?"

"If the weather and the Roadster hold up, I think it should work out. Maybe something will happen today."

At three-thirty, there was a knock on the door. It was Al, the highway patrol officer who had worked Duke's crash site yesterday. He was sent to assist the Feds Immediately. Others would join the team as soon as possible, fulfilling Jerry's request.

Minutes later, the third member of Jerry's team arrived.

"We've located Augie," he reported as he came inside. He explained that his partner had stayed behind to escort Augie back to Los Angeles.

With everyone around the kitchen table, Ida served coffee and homemade apple pie.

Jerry brought everyone up to speed.

Jerry said, "Our plan to capture these guys is very simple. They believe Marty has the money. And he's volunteered to show his face around Santa Rosaria today and, if necessary tomorrow, to draw them out. Because the diner in town is the only public place to eat, we're going to focus our efforts there.

"As for the trap, Marty will drive into Santa Rosaria and go directly to the diner, parking his car in a spot highly visible from the highway. Then, if those four show up, we take them.

The plan called for the third Fed to remain behind, to turn over the money to the agents from L.A. and insure instructions were followed. Jerry and Elliott would follow Marty into town. Al, the state cop, was to be the backstop for the unforeseen.

"Okay, let's go round up the bad guys," Jerry said.

# 21

$M$arty cruised into Santa Rosaria full of hope. Taking down the four from L.A. would assure a quiet trip home.

Suddenly everything changed. There was Cathy, about to pull out of the gas station! No mistake, it was her! And she saw him! Blasting onto the highway, she locked onto the Roadster. She even took up the Feds following position, by inadvertently forcing them off the road.

He was astonished as he watched the skidding car disappear into a dust cloud.

How the hell did she know they were Feds? he wondered. At the next residential street he turned left and circled the block. Instead of going back onto Route 66, where the Roadster had little chance of survival, he turned into a large parking lot.

The lot served about a dozen shops and stores, and several dozen parked cars were widely scattered across the large area. The chase through the parked cars lasted for a few minutes, before Cathy lost control of her car and plowed into what was probably the heaviest car on the lot.

Rushing to her aid, Marty found her head had penetrated the windshield. Seconds later, Elliott joined in the rescue, followed by Al, who came to a screeching halt alongside the wreck. Working together, the three men freed her from the windshield. She was covered in blood and still unconscious.

"We've got to get her to the hospital in Beckonall," Al said.

The siren screamed as they raced out of the parking area and turned onto Route 66. As the minutes passed, Marty couldn't help thinking back over the past week to Cathy's senseless, violent acts. This time she'd really done it. How would Mary and Patrick handle the news if she doesn't survive this? he wondered.

The hospital was now in sight. Cathy was quickly placed on a gurney and rushed inside.

Al, Elliott and Marty went to the men's room to get cleaned up. Back outside in the hallway, Marty turned to Al. "Could you do me a big favor and check on my car? You're not going to believe this, but I left the keys in it."

"I'll get right on it."

Soon after, a doctor came out. "She's a fighter," the doctor said. "If she pulls through this, she has you men to thank. We've notified her father."

Knowing there was nothing further they could do, the three left for Santa Rosaria.

A few minutes outside Beckonall, the radio crackled. The voice said, "I remember seeing that old Ford, when I reached the accident scene earlier, Al, but it's not here now. Nobody's here now."

But that can't be! Marty thought. "Jerry was supposed to ..." Then it hit him. The Fed's car was forced off the road and must have been disabled.

In little more than twenty-four hours, Cathy and Duke were hospitalized, all that remained of the Nomad and trailer were memories and, now, the backbreaker, his lost Roadster. In a nutshell, the Roadster project had crashed and burned.

Why the hell did I give Duke a ride yesterday? he asked himself. Why didn't I disarm him? I had chances. And, why did I go to the hospital? There were others who could have done that.

The pain of his failures cascaded down on him. For once, he had no plans, no ideas, on what to do next.

In fact, Jerry had moved to a good position for surveillance, some distance from the lunacy in the parking lot. With the excitement over and the businesses closing for the day, the parking lot was now mostly empty.

Soon after dark, a white truck pulled up near the Roadster. The speed and ease with which the thieves loaded the old car into their truck was amazing. Moments later, the truck pulled out and turned west on Route 66.

Jerry immediately called the highway patrol. After identifying himself, he asked that their nearest officer make a stolen car arrest. He would provide the backup.

"Please tell your officer to wait until he's at least five miles from Santa Rosaria, before taking any action," Jerry said.

Trailing the truck, Jerry asked to be connected with Al. "Al, this is Jerry. I'm following a white furniture truck with Marty's car inside. At the moment, I'm a few miles west of Santa Rosaria. Once one of your officers gets here, we're going to move in."

"Jerry, I got a guy here who's trying to rip the phone out of my hand," Al said.

"Marty, your car is fine. Don't worry. You'd better get your butt out here, though, because I'm fighting the temptation of taking it for a spin," Jerry quipped.

Jerry watched as a patrol car raced past from the opposite direction. A minute later it had turned around and come up from behind. The patrol car slowed and came alongside. Jerry signaled and the patrol car surged ahead.

Charlie and Morg offered no resistance and had already been searched for weapons and handcuffed by the time Marty and the others arrived.

Marty took a look at the thieves and turned to Jerry, shaking his head. "Who are these guys?"

"They're not talking. All we know so far is their names and that they're residents of Chastaine, California." Jerry answered.

"No, it can't be," he said, shaking his head.

"You know these people?" Jerry asked.

Marty told of the offer to buy the Roadster.

"And you didn't sell? Another Roadster, just like yours, and five thousand dollars?"

"It's kind of hard to explain."

After the car was unloaded, Marty asked Jerry to ride with him back to Ida and Chet's place.

On the way, Jerry asked, "Okay, who was that crazy woman who tried to scatter you and this car all over the parking lot? And why?"

Marty explained as best he could.

"She came all this way, because you disappointed her?"

Marty responded with a nod.

"Damn! What do you think will happen to her?"

"Well, the highway patrol has a full day's worth of paperwork to process against her," Jerry replied. "She won't be bothering you for quite some time, I suspect."

"Maybe it was a miracle, but she didn't hurt anyone today, really. She needs professional help, my friend. Can you do anything for her?"

"It's not my call, Marty. I'll try."

They were soon turning onto the familiar dirt road and it wasn't long before Ida had a hot meal for the men before she and Chet went off to bed.

While they ate, Jerry said, "The money bag was dusted for prints, right here on the table. Augie's prints were all over it. He's ours!"

Turning to Marty, he said, "You ready to wrap this up tomorrow?"

"I am. Only this time there's no way in hell that car will get out of my sight tomorrow. Thanks for getting it back for me."

Marty was awake for only a short time, but before he drifted off, a smile came over his face when he thought about his Roadster tucked away safely in the barn.

# 22

**M**arty was up early and removed his Roadster from the barn. By early afternoon he would be on the road for home. His only hope of not facing those four guys from L.A., on the way home, was to apprehend them this morning, while he had help.

He parked the Roadster in the middle of the diner's parking lot, in clear view of passersby. There was no sign of the black Buick. Inside, he found a dozen patrons seated at the counter and tables. Taking a seat at the counter, he ordered breakfast.

His thoughts returned to the Roadster and the pending trip home. In particular, the time it was going to take to complete the trip was troubling. Suppose he runs into weather? he wondered. Suppose he's only in Ohio, when time runs out? What then? What's he to do with the Roadster? And, how could he possibly justify his tardiness in reporting for duty, in view of the exceedingly generous time-off he was allowed by Captain Wilson? Was this to ultimately come down to a choice between a long stint in Wilson's doghouse, maybe worse, or the Roadster's preservation? And Margie, what about her?

After pondering the problem for a time, he made a very difficult decision. When he returned the ranch, he would ask Chet if he could leave the Roadster in his care until he could come for it, in three or four months. He would ask Jerry for a ride to the airport, in Albuquerque, and fly home. Roadster problem solved. Even so, the idea of leaving his treasure behind soured him.

By nine-thirty, he was on his fourth cup of coffee, when he noticed the diner had been mostly vacated. He and two other customers were all that remained.

Still working on the Margie situation, the door opened and in walked the L.A. four, who took seats on both sides of him.

"That's a real nice car you've got out there," George said.

"Yeah, thanks."

"That was one helluva show you two put on in the parking lot yesterday. Glad you and the old car came out of it so well."

"Me to," Marty said with a smile.

"We've been hoping to have a word with you."

"I figured."

The man behind the counter had just finished filling the cups of the four, when Marty nodded toward the tables and carried his coffee over to one. The others followed.

When everyone was seated, Marty stood up and turned completely around. "I'm not armed," he said, reaching for his wallet. Sitting down, he removed his state police I.D. card and handed it to George.

"I was out in L.A., when I met that guy Duke," Marty said. After briefly explaining his involvement with Duke, he told how he came into possession of the robbery money.

"Once I found the money, I called the U.S. Treasury people, in L.A. You know, it being their money and all. They showed up a few hours later. I also passed along the information Duke gave me about your friend, Augie, and approximately where he was being treated for the leg injury. Now the Feds have him. They've already moved him back to L.A."

The four men looked very concerned and exchanged nervous glances.

"I'm guessing you'd be George Arliss," Marty said to George. And then he rattled off the names of the others, in no particular order.

Marty gestured to the parking lot. "They intend to arrest you guys, too. Peacefully, I hope."

All four moved to the window to discover the three Feds and four highway patrol cars spread around the parking lot.

"I'm supposed to tell you that the highway patrol has the highway locked down."

The men returned to the table, but remained standing.

"You know," Marty continued, "if this situation turned into something crazy and a cop gets killed ... well, I understand that New Mexico would treat all of you, uh, special."

The men continued to stare at him.

"If you fellas would let me walk out that door with all of your weapons, speaking as a cop, it would sure work in your favor, later on."

After a long pause, George placed his gun on the table. Two of the others followed suit. The lone hold-out backed off a few paces, but two of his associates forcefully disarmed him and tossed the gun to Marty.

George motioned to the guns on the table and said, "The guns aren't loaded. They've never been fired. Ever."

Afterwards, Marty drove to the highway patrol office in Beckonall to complete the paperwork on the Nomad's theft, to satisfy his insurance company.

While in town, he stopped off at the hospital to see Cathy and find out how Duke was doing. Apparently both would eventually be capable of doing whatever jail time, if any, they might draw.

A little past noon, he'd returned to the ranch. To his surprise, a large truck, complete with driver, waited to transport him and his car to Pennsylvania. According to Jerry, the service was being provided, compliments of a grateful U.S. Treasury Department.

With the Feds ready to pull out, Jerry took Marty aside.

"Marty, I have a favor to ask. Would you give some thought to joining our organization, as an agent?"

Marty looked surprised, but then smiled.

"I'll be in touch in a week or so and we'll explore some things.

"In the meantime, I expect to be spending a good deal of time with Augie. I understand he continues to be very co-operative," Jerry said.

"The two men talked for another minute or so, before Marty hurried over to the truck.

After driving the Roadster inside the truck, he helped the driver secure his treasure.

Then he joined Ida and Chet.

"How do I thank you folks for saving my life?" he said, while shaking Chet's hand.

Hugging Ida, he continued, "And without your help, who knows how things might have turned out."

"Anyone would have done the same thing," Chet said quietly. "We're the ones thanking you, Marty. That surprise reward money, well, it'll give us and this old place a new lease on life."

Ida kissed his cheek. "If you're ever out this way, stop in and see us, Marty."

"You bet I will."

# 23

Marty stood in the middle of the dirt road and watched, as the truck drove off to Pennsylvania with his Roadster. He was sure this was the last time he would see the old car for at least the next three or four months. When it was out of sight, he hooked his thumbs in the back pockets of his khaki's and slowly walked to the waiting car.

Getting in, he said, "Thanks for the ride, Jerry."

Riding home with his treasure was a big deal for Marty, but seeing Margie before he left for his new assignment was so much bigger. And the only way that could happen was to fly from Albuquerque, directly to New York City.

Once there, he would buy a ring, find her, and propose. Within the hour, he'd head for Carlisle, see his folks, while he packed, ask his dad to look after the Roadster when it arrived, then hurry off in his '51 Ford. With some decent weather, he just might get to the other side of the state to report for duty, on time.

If all went well with Margie, he'd call her when the dust settled and ask her to consider Niagara Falls, as their honeymoon destination. Their Roadster could do the trip without breaking a sweat.